"I don't regret anything that happened last night," Cecilia said.

Geoff reached out to cover her hand with his. "It was one of the best nights I've had in a very long time."

She laced her fingers with his. "For me, too."

"So what's the problem?"

"I'm sort of afraid of ruining everything now."

"Not possible."

"You haven't heard what I want to ask you yet." In response to Geoff's wary expression Cecilia laughed a little and held up her hands. "Relax. I'm not asking you to marry me. Our night together hasn't turned me into a starry-eyed romantic with dreams of a happily-ever-after."

"So what is this request?"

She drew a deep breath, then blurted the words before she lost her nerve. "I want you to help me make a baby."

Dear Reader,

It's that time of year again—when every woman's thoughts turn to love—and we have all kinds of romantic gifts for you! We begin with the latest from reader favorite Allison Leigh, *Secretly Married,* in which she concludes her popular TURNABOUT miniseries. A woman who was sure she was divorced finds out there's the little matter of her not-so-ex-husband's signing the papers, so off she goes to Turnabout—the island that can turn your life around—to get her divorce. Or does she?

Our gripping MERLYN COUNTY MIDWIVES miniseries continues with Gina Wilkins's *Countdown to Baby.* A woman interested only in baby-making—or so she thinks—may be finding happily-ever-after *and* her little bundle of joy, with the town's most eligible bachelor. LOGAN'S LEGACY, our new Silhouette continuity, is introduced in *The Virgin's Makeover* by Judy Duarte, in which a plain-Jane adoptee is transformed in time to find her inner beauty…and, just possibly, her biological family. Look for the next installment in this series coming next month. Shirley Hailstock's *Love on Call* tells the story of two secretive emergency-room doctors who find temptation—not to mention danger—in each other. In *Down from the Mountain* by Barbara Gale, two disabled people—a woman without sight, and a scarred man—nonetheless find each other a perfect match. And Arlene James continues THE RICHEST GALS IN TEXAS with *Fortune Finds Florist.* A sudden windfall turns complicated when a wealthy small-town florist forms a business relationship—for starters—with a younger man who has more than finance on his mind.

So Happy Valentine's Day, and don't forget to join us next month, for six special romances, all from Silhouette Special Edition.

Sincerely,

Gail Chasan
Senior Editor

Please address questions and book requests to:
Silhouette Reader Service
U.S.: 3010 Walden Ave., P.O. Box 1325, Buffalo, NY 14269
Canadian: P.O. Box 609, Fort Erie, Ont. L2A 5X3

Countdown
to Baby

GINA WILKINS

Silhouette

SPECIAL EDITION®

Published by Silhouette Books

America's Publisher of Contemporary Romance

Special thanks and acknowledgment are given to Gina Wilkins for her contribution to the MERLYN COUNTY MIDWIVES series.

For Sally—she of the untapped wisdom.

SILHOUETTE BOOKS

ISBN 0-373-24592-0

COUNTDOWN TO BABY

Copyright © 2004 by Harlequin Books S.A.

This edition published by arrangement with Harlequin Books S.A.

® and TM are trademarks of Harlequin Books S.A., used under license. Trademarks indicated with ® are registered in the United States Patent and Trademark Office, the Canadian Trade Marks Office and in other countries.

Visit Silhouette at www.eHarlequin.com

Printed in U.S.A.

Books by Gina Wilkins

Silhouette Special Edition

The Father Next Door #1082
It Could Happen To You #1119
Valentine Baby #1153
†*Her Very Own Family* #1243
†*That First Special Kiss* #1269
Surprise Partners #1318
***The Stranger in Room 205* #1399
***Bachelor Cop Finally
    Caught?* #1413
***Dateline Matrimony* #1424
The Groom's Stand-In #1460
The Best Man's Plan #1479
*The Family Plan #1525
**Conflict of Interest* #1531
**Faith, Hope and Family* #1538
Make-Believe Mistletoe #1583
Countdown to Baby #1592

Silhouette Books

World's Most Eligible Bachelors
Doctor in Disguise

†Family Found: Sons & Daughters
**Hot Off the Press
§Family Found
‡The Family Way
*The McClouds of Mississippi

**Previously published
as Gina Ferris**

Silhouette Special Edition

Healing Sympathy #496
Lady Beware #549
In from the Rain #677
Prodigal Father #711
§*Full of Grace* #793
§*Hardworking Man* #806
§*Fair and Wise* #819
§*Far To Go* #862
§*Loving and Giving* #879
Babies on Board #913

**Previously published
as Gina Ferris Wilkins**

Silhouette Special Edition

‡*A Man for Mom* #955
‡*A Match for Celia* #967
‡*A Home for Adam* #980
‡*Cody's Fiancée* #1006

Silhouette Books

Mother's Day Collection 1995
Three Mothers and a Cradle
    "Beginnings"

GINA WILKINS

is a bestselling and award-winning author who has written more than sixty-five books for Harlequin and Silhouette. She credits her successful career in romance to her long, happy marriage and her three "extraordinary" children.

A lifelong resident of central Arkansas, Ms. Wilkins sold her first book to Harlequin in 1987 and has been writing full-time since. She has appeared on the Waldenbooks, B. Dalton and *USA TODAY* bestseller lists. She is a three-time recipient of the Maggie Award for Excellence, sponsored by Georgia Romance Writers, and has won several awards from the reviewers of *Romantic Times*.

Merlyn County Regional
Hospital Happenings

Welcome to Lily Cunningham, public relations director extraordinaire! Lily's experience—from dining with royalty to saving billion-dollar corporations—is sure to bring prestige to our hospital and the new biomedical research facility sponsored by Dr. Mari Bingham. If you see Lily in the halls—she'll be wearing her signature color: red—give her a warm Kentucky hello!

Congratulations to Eric Mendoza on his promotion—and his engagement to expectant mother Hannah Bingham!

If anyone has seen *any* strange behavior at the Foster Clinic or in the pharmacy department of the hospital in the last few weeks, please report this to Dr. Mari Bingham or her receptionist *immediately!*

And thanks to midwife Cecilia Mendoza for her hard work and dedication to the Foster Clinic. Please congratulate her on ten years of caring for Merlyn County's mothers and babies!

Chapter One

The slippery seven-pound boy squirmed in Cecilia Mendoza's arms. Pink legs flailed with his irritation at being shoved out of his warm, liquid cocoon and into the openness and light of the clinic birthing room. A series of shrill screams issued from his toothless mouth, and his scrunched face was beet red with fury.

Cecilia thought he was absolutely beautiful. With hidden reluctance, she transferred the child into the arms of his exhausted but eager mother. The stocky young father hovered close by, his ruddy face split with an enormous, proud, and just a bit nervous, smile.

Pushing her own emotions to the back of her mind, Cecilia concentrated on her job as a certified nurse midwife, turning her attention to the routine follow-up procedures of this blessedly complication-free delivery. Her workday was almost over. She couldn't go straight home, unfortunately, because of the reception for Lillith Cunningham, the new public relations director for the Foster Midwifery Clinic and the Bingham Midwifery School, both affiliated with the regional hospital in Merlyn County, Kentucky. The reception was to begin at six. Cecilia wasn't particularly looking forward to the event, but she felt obligated to drop in.

She could contemplate her feelings of wistfulness, envy and frustration later, when she was alone in her house, longing for a child of her own. As her thirty-eighth birthday loomed closer, she couldn't help wondering if she would ever know the joy of holding her own baby.

Geoff Bingham's bedroom smelled of freshly applied orange-oil wood polish and a hint of woodlands-scented air freshener. As he precisely knotted an expensive red silk tie around the neck of his tailored white shirt, he wondered if he was only imagining the slightly musty scent of a long-unoccupied room beneath the more pleasing fragrances.

His efficient housekeeper made sure his condo was always clean and welcoming when he returned from one of his many long business trips, but sometimes the place still felt foreign to him. Like just another of the series of hotel suites and corporate apartments he slept in during his travels—when his demanding job allowed him to sleep, of course.

Picking up the hand-tailored jacket that had been laid out on his bed, he shrugged into it as automatically as a mechanic might don his blue cotton work shirt. As far as Geoff was concerned, this fifteen-hundred-dollar suit was merely a business uniform, no more indicative of his true personality than his immaculately polished wing-tip shoes. The party for which he was dressing was just another business meeting to him, at which he would smile and mingle and shake hands with the smooth skill he had spent the past ten of his thirty-two years developing.

Squeezing the tight muscles at the back of his neck with his left hand, he could only hope the reception for the hospital's new public relations director wouldn't last long. All he wanted to do was get this over with, come back to his citrus-scented condo and crash in the den with a beer, some chips and his treasured Taylor guitar. An evening of quiet solitude sounded very good to him right now. But he would do his duty. He always did.

"So, Geoff." A florid-faced man in a suit that was too tight across the belly clapped him on the back with enough force to make him almost stagger. "How long are you in town for this time?"

With the benefit of a decade of practice, Geoff held on to his pleasant smile, which was, to him, as much a tool of his trade as a hammer was to a carpenter. "Looks like I could be around for a while this time."

"That's good to hear." Bob Howard slapped Geoff's back again. "Maybe we can hit the golf course. Not this weekend, I'm afraid. The wife's sister is coming for a visit, and I'm expected to entertain my moron of a brother-in-law."

That was one thing Geoff could identify with. Family obligations. His entire life revolved around them. "Maybe some other time."

"I'll give you a call."

Geoff could think of a couple dozen things he would rather do than spend an afternoon golfing with Bob Howard—root canals and ditch digging among them—but since Howard's bank was a major financier for Bingham Enterprises, he spoke warmly. "I'll look forward to it."

Howard moved on, and Geoff took advantage of the moment of peace to take another bracing swallow of his lemonade. Around him various members of his family—his father, his grandmother, his sister, his cousins—worked the crowd attending the reception for the new public relations director for Merlyn County Regional Hospital.

The hospital had been founded by Geoff's grandparents and was still family controlled, along with their other local and international business interests. The Binghams took their responsibilities to the corporation and to the community very seriously. And to the rest of the family, of course.

Even Geoff's late, wild, uncle Billy's illegitimate offspring—the ones he had acknowledged, anyway—had certain expectations thrust upon them, whether they wanted them or not. Two of those cousins, Dr. Kyle Bingham and Hannah Bingham-soon-to-be-Mendoza, were in attendance at this affair, doing their part to promote the hospital and its upcoming public relations campaign.

Geoff's gaze lingered on Hannah, who was several

months along in her pregnancy. She had very recently announced her engagement to Eric Mendoza, a rising young executive in Bingham Enterprises. The couple looked radiantly happy, and the engagement had been approved by Geoff's father and grandmother.

In their opinions, Hannah needed someone to help her raise the child she had conceived in an ill-advised affair several months ago, and young Eric needed a wife to help him further his career. This marriage was the ideal solution, as far as they were concerned.

It wouldn't be long, Geoff feared, before they turned their attentions back to him. Ever since his thirtieth birthday two years ago, they had been pressuring him to find a suitable bride and start producing more Binghams.

While Geoff had no problem with the idea of fatherhood, the prospect of marriage did not appeal to him at all. As it was now, his free time was almost nonexistent. The opportunities were extremely rare for him to do whatever he felt like doing without taking anyone else's needs or wishes into consideration. In his opinion, a wife was simply someone else who would claim a right to his time and attention.

Maybe he could subtly redirect the family's matchmaking efforts to his sister Mari, he mused. After all, she was thirty-four and firmly established as an M.D. and director of the Foster Midwifery Clinic and the Bingham Midwifery School. Sure, she was busy with her duties and her plans for the biomedical research center she dreamed of founding here in town, but she was no busier than Geoff, whose primary job was to secure funding for those grandiose plans and to keep the other Bingham Enterprises interests viable in an increasingly tough international market.

Someone walked by nibbling on a fat, juicy-looking chocolate-dipped strawberry, reminding Geoff he hadn't eaten in a while. He glanced toward the refreshments tables, where a small crowd of attendees munched on summer party fare. His gaze lingered on a beautiful brunette in a flame red dress.

Cecilia Mendoza. A prominent midwife at the clinic, Eric's sister was an extremely attractive woman Geoff had admired several times but had never actually met.

Maybe he would sample the treats before he made his escape from this boring affair.

The reception was held in the atrium of the administration and education building on the hospital campus. Four stories high, the fully enclosed atrium was a haven of glass, greenery, statuary and fountains. Wrought-iron tables, chairs and benches were scattered artfully around the stone floors. Greenery cascaded from the balconies of the floors above, leading the eye to the angled glass roof high above their heads. Accessed by gently rising ramps, another balcony circled the main atrium, holding more tables and chairs and providing a second level for entertaining and activities.

There was very little empty space, Cecilia noted as she entered the atrium from the back hallway that led into the main clinic building. When Mari Bingham arranged an official event, few members of her staff or the surrounding business community failed to make an appearance.

This affair had been billed as an informal after-hours welcome for the new PR director. Cecilia was a bit late because she had taken the time to change out of her wilted scrubs and into a bright red sheath dress she'd chosen to counter the weariness of a long day's work. Sleeveless and scoop-necked, it fit closely to her hips, then flared out just a little and fell to her knees.

She had reluctantly swapped her comfortable walking shoes for a pair of black high-heeled sandals, and her feet were already protesting. Several tendrils of dark hair had escaped the upswept style she had worn for convenience, tickling the back of her neck and her freshly made-up cheeks when she turned her head to greet friends and business associates who had already gathered around the refreshments tables.

In deference to the heat of a July evening, the caterers served frosty lemonade, iced raspberry tea and light snacks—chilled shrimp, crisp vegetables, tiny sandwiches, fresh fruits and flaky pastries. Cecilia looked longingly at the food. She had worked through her usual lunchtime—the McAllister baby having chosen just then to make her appearance—and she was hungry. But since she had never quite mastered the art of eating, mingling and conversing all at the same time, she settled for a clear-plastic tumbler of lemonade and a single chocolate-dipped strawberry, which she barely had time to eat before a deep, masculine voice spoke from close behind her.

''I don't know about you, but I wish they'd served

pizza and cheeseburgers. It would take a whole platter full of these little munchies to fill me up.''

Uncertain if he was talking to her, she turned her head to make sure. She found herself looking straight into the clear hazel eyes of Geoff Bingham, a top executive of Bingham Enterprises and brother to the administrator of the clinic where Cecilia had spent her entire career as a certified nurse midwife.

She identified him immediately, of course—few people in these parts would not—but she had never actually spoken to him before. ''I think it would be hard to gracefully eat pizza and cheeseburgers standing in a crowd of dressed-up people,'' she replied in the same light tone he had used. And then she smiled. ''But it does sound good.''

Geoff studied the selection of finger foods spread on the tables and shook his head. ''It all looks very nice, but there's no real food here. I've got to talk to Mari about putting out buckets of chicken or stacks of burritos or something for the next official event.''

Cecilia couldn't help but laugh at the image of this restrained and proper crowd munching on chicken legs and burritos. ''I'm sure that's going to happen.''

His gaze drifted down to her mouth. ''So, do you have any recommendations for a guy who's very close to starvation?''

He was definitely flirting with her, and she wasn't too tired to appreciate the attentions of such a handsome and charming man. It had been too long since she had been studied with such open masculine approval—and not in an insulting way, she decided, but decidedly flattering. This brief exchange would give her something to smile about later while she was sitting alone in her house with her feet up and a cup of coffee beside her.

She glanced at the tables again before answering him. "I don't see anything particularly filling here, but I can recommend the strawberries. The one I had was delicious."

He reached past her to pluck one of the chocolate-dipped berries from a serving platter. His arm almost, but not quite, brushed against her with the movement. Close enough to make her pulse trip a bit, in a very pleasant way. She couldn't help watching as he took a bite of the fruit, and she found herself moistening her own lips with the tip of her tongue.

Goodness, but this was one fine-looking man.

"You're right," he told her, his voice low and intimate, as if they were the only ones present in this crowded room. "This is good. Want a bite?"

The blatant entendre earned him a look of reprimand, and then a smile she made no effort to repress. "Thanks, but I've already had one."

"A woman of great willpower, I see."

Cecilia gave him a look from beneath her eyelashes. "When I choose to be."

His left eyebrow rose. "So…"

"Geoff. Hey, Geoff, good to see you." A balding man whose suit hung loosely on his bony physique peered over the tops of half glasses as he spoke, seemingly unaware of Cecilia's presence.

Recognizing the newcomer as a prominent local business owner, and guessing Geoff was there specifically to mingle with potential investors in Mari's planned biomedical research center, Cecilia tactfully slipped away. She was still smiling when she joined a group of her co-workers in another corner of the room.

"Was that Geoff Bingham you were flirting with over there?" Vanessa Harris, a registered nurse, instructor, and Cecilia's closest friend in the clinic, asked.

"Unless you know some other rich, movie-star-gorgeous guy that might have made an appearance here today," Cecilia quipped in return.

"Well, did you slip him your phone number?"

"Gee, I would have, but you know my policy. I never date men who are prettier than I am."

Vanessa laughed, and, after a moment, Cecilia joined in. As much as she had dreaded this reception, it was surprisingly enjoyable. Amazing what a few minutes of flirting with a handsome man and laughing with a friend could do to turn around a trying day.

"Have you met the new PR director yet?" Vanessa asked in a low voice.

Cecilia stopped casting what she hoped were discreet looks toward the man still standing near the food tables and turned back to her friend. "No. Have you?"

Vanessa's nod made her trademark large hoop earrings sway against her cheeks. "This afternoon."

Tall and lushly rounded, Vanessa was a striking woman who would stand out in any crowd, even if it weren't for her penchant for brightly colored clothing. She wore her black hair cropped close to her head. Her nearly black eyes glittered with a sharp wit and avid interest in her surroundings, and her flawless, chocolate-toned skin was taut and smooth. Having noted the faintest hint of developing laugh lines around her own brown eyes and full mouth, Cecilia could only hope she would look as good when she was forty-five.

Vanessa's attractiveness wasn't all Cecilia envied. Her friend was also the mother of four delightful children—two boys and twin girls, all under twelve. Vanessa was even lucky enough to have found one of those rare men who was deeply committed to his family and would probably stay with them through thick and thin, unlike so many of the men Cecilia had encountered.

"What did you think of Lillith Cunningham?" she asked, trying to put her growing obsession with children and motherhood out of her mind for the remainder of the evening—or at least until she got home.

"She's interesting," Vanessa replied. "Kind of artsy looking, you know? Flowing clothes in bright colors, jingling jewelry. No doubt she comes from money, but she's got a nice smile, so maybe the wealth hasn't gone to her head."

"Mari wouldn't hire a snob to promote the clinic," Cecilia said, confident that she was right. Dr. Mari Bingham certainly fit the description of a woman who had been raised in wealth and privilege, but she still knew how to work hard and mingle comfortably with people of all circumstances. Anyone who wanted to adequately represent the Foster Midwifery Clinic, with its huge diversity of patients and associates, would have to possess the same qualities.

"You're probably right. Mari's a good judge of character—most of the time," Vanessa added in a mutter.

Their conversation was interrupted when Milla Johnson, a young midwifery student, greeted them quietly. Pretty and competent, Milla was one of the shining stars of the midwifery school, and Cecilia had grown quite fond of her. She couldn't help noticing that Milla looked a bit tired this evening, despite what appeared to be a fresh application of blusher and lip-stick.

Milla was definitely showing the effects of the strain of her demanding job, in addition to the worry of a malpractice lawsuit that Cecilia considered little more than an unfair nuisance by a couple determined to blame their own shortcomings on someone else. Milla, in this case.

"Have you had anything to eat lately?" she asked the younger woman in rather maternal concern. "You look a little pale."

"I'm fine," Milla replied, trying to smile. "It's just been a long day."

"Tell me about it," Cecilia agreed with a crooked grin, pressing a hand to her back to indicate her own weariness. "We're well into a Merlyn County baby boom, aren't we?"

Milla chuckled wearily. "I think the population of Binghamton almost doubled in the past week alone."

"We've sure got a boatload of Binghams repre-sented here tonight," Vanessa murmured in a bit of a non sequitur as she surveyed the crowded room. "There's dear Miss Myrtle and Mr. Ron. And Mari and Geoff. You know this event's a big deal if they brought him home for it. Then there's Hannah, of course, I suppose she counts as a Bingham. Don't she and your brother look happy, Cecilia?''

Cecilia smiled mistily across the room to where her handsome and utterly adored younger brother, Eric, stood attentively next to a lovely, and very pregnant, Hannah. The couple were so visibly in love—and so excited about the child they would soon welcome into their lives.

Eric was another exception to Cecilia's general theory that most men weren't interested in long-term family obligations. There was no question in her mind that Eric's commitment to Hannah and her baby would last a lifetime.

And as happy as she was for her brother, she couldn't help envying...

"Oops. Almost missed a Bingham," Vanessa added cheerily. "Dr. Kyle is posed broodingly on the other side of the atrium, looking like he stepped off a *GQ* cover. He is one fine-looking young man, isn't he?''

Cecilia's smile deepened. ''If you happen to appreciate blond hair, blue eyes, a pretty face and a perfect body. And who doesn't, right, Milla?''

Her formerly pale face now bright pink, Milla murmured an answer, then made an excuse to move away. Something about seeing someone she needed to speak to.

With a slight frown, Cecilia watched Milla hurry away. Like others who worked closely with them, she hadn't missed the sparks between the young nurse and

Dr. Kyle Bingham. But something other than a possibly complicated attraction seemed to be haunting Milla, and, worrier that she was, it concerned her. "Does it seem to you that Milla's been acting oddly lately, Van?"

"Who wouldn't be, with that stupid lawsuit hanging over her? But she'll be okay, don't you worry. Mari and the legal staff will take good care of her."

"I'm sure you're right." Telling herself to let the experts worry about Milla's problems, Cecilia glanced discreetly at her functional, easily readable stainless steel watch. "Wonder how soon before we can make an escape? I'm ready to get home and crash."

"I'll try not to take that as a comment on my sparkling companionship."

Smiling, Cecilia shook her head. "Like Milla, I'm just tired. It really has been a long day."

"I'm about ready to head home, myself. George is supposed to have the kids fed and homework supervised, but you know how it goes. I'll probably have to check to make sure it all got done. And I want to read Damien his bedtime story tonight."

Vanessa couldn't have known, of course, that her lighthearted words would go straight to Cecilia's heart. Though Vanessa knew Cecilia wanted children of her own, she had no idea just how strong that longing had become.

It was with some relief that Cecilia was able to change the subject of the conversation. "I think someone wants to speak to you," she said, nodding toward a young nursing student who was trying to get

Vanessa's attention. "Looks like a lively discussion is going on over there."

Vanessa sighed. "I'm sure there is. That group is always getting into a debate about something—and I always seem to get called in as referee."

"Mama Vanessa," Cecilia teased. "Go take care of your chicks. I'm going to try to score another chocolate-dipped strawberry."

"Okay. Catch you later." Vanessa moved to the group of nursing students and was soon engaged in an animated conversation with them.

Cecilia worked her way slowly across the crowded atrium, pausing several times to chat with co-workers. She made sure she spoke to enough people to leave no doubt that she had attended the gathering—standard office politics. On the other side of the room, her brother and his fiancée were surrounded by well-wishers. She managed to swap smiles and waves with them, but she made no effort to join them. As a rising young executive in the Bingham corporation, Eric had his own politics to practice this evening.

And, speaking of Binghams...

She smiled when Geoff stepped in front of her again. "Still looking for a cheeseburger, Mr. Bingham?"

He chuckled. "Actually, I'm hungry enough now for a thick slab of steak and a huge baked potato. These little finger foods aren't going to hold me any longer."

"I know what you mean. I haven't had time to eat since breakfast this morning."

"So, how about it? Want to go find a steak?"

She blinked. "Um...now?"

"Of course. We're both hungry. We've dutifully made our appearances at this official reception thing, and there's no reason for either of us to stay any longer. So, if you have no plans for the remainder of the evening, I would be honored if you would join me for dinner."

She could hardly believe that Geoff Bingham was impulsively asking her out within a few minutes of meeting her. Heck, she couldn't even say they had met, officially. She was quite sure she hadn't even told him her name. "We haven't even been introduced."

His grin deepened, pushing intriguing creases into his lean cheeks. "We haven't, have we? Of course you already know I'm Geoff Bingham, and I know you're Eric Mendoza's sister, Cecilia. You're a valuable member of the midwifery team here and highly respected by everyone who mentions you. I'd like to get a chance to know you myself."

So he did know who she was. Maybe, she decided, he just didn't like eating alone. Maybe he was using her as an excuse to get out of this reception—being the gentleman by feeding a hungry guest, being a good executive by getting to know one of the subordinates in the organization, getting better acquainted with the sister of the man who was marrying one of his cousins. All sorts of rationales could apply. The question was, did she want to accept?

Rather surprisingly, considering her earlier weariness and eagerness to get home, the answer was yes.

Maybe she was simply trying to postpone going

home alone—again—to contemplate her life and her future. Maybe watching Eric and Hannah from across the room made her aware again of her own depressing lack of a social life, if she discounted a few disastrous blind dates—which she did. Or maybe she simply liked the idea of spending a couple of hours with an attractive, charming and interesting man.

Deciding she had no reason at all to turn him down, she smiled. "Would you mind if I order chicken instead of steak?"

Satisfaction gleamed in his clear hazel eyes. "That can definitely be arranged."

Chapter Two

If he had known when he'd dressed for the evening that he would end up dining with a beautiful brunette, he wouldn't have been so reluctant to attend the reception, Geoff mused as he studied Cecilia Mendoza across a cozy table a short time later. Melinda's was busy this evening, as it was most weekends, but a combination of clever table arrangement and discreet lighting gave them a sense of privacy as they studied the menus by candlelight.

At Cecilia's suggestion, they had left the reception separately, driving their own cars to the restaurant. He had assumed the suggestion was based at least partly on discretion, since the gossip lines in the clinic were as active as in any tight-knit work environment. He had to admit it had been clever of her.

Geoff had had the foresight to call ahead as he'd

left the hospital so that a table had been waiting for them, avoiding the usual lengthy wait for seating. He didn't often wield his influence as a member of one of the wealthiest and most prominent local families, but this had been one of the rare occasions when it had been irresistible to do so. If Cecilia had been impressed, she hadn't let it show, which was something else he liked about her.

"I think I'll have the trout," she said, laying her menu aside.

"Change your mind about the chicken?"

Her smile brought out tiny dimples at the corners of her mouth. Geoff couldn't keep from staring at them as she replied, "Actually, everything looks so good it's hard to decide. It's been quite a while since I've had the chance to dine here."

He dragged his gaze back up to her eyes. "Then I'm glad you were free to join me tonight."

Located in an old firehouse, Melinda's was a steak and seafood restaurant with a menu and a wine list that compared favorably to anything in the state, as far as Geoff was concerned. He liked the history of the place, the redbrick walls decorated with framed black-and-white vintage photographs from Merlyn County's colorful past, the polished brass pole left over from the old fire station, the huge carved oak bar that made up the entire back wall of the popular lounge downstairs.

Geoff's family had always come here for special occasions, such as birthdays and anniversaries, and the management had always given them preferential treatment. During the past few years, he had dined in some of the most renowned restaurants in the world, but Melinda's would always feel like home to him.

Having placed their orders with the server who had been hovering discreetly nearby, Geoff focused on his companion again. "I'm told the clinic has been very busy lately."

Her smile turned wry. "You're told correctly. We've decided there's a major baby boom going on in Merlyn County. And there's more and more demand for midwifery services, partially due to the shortage of obstetricians in the county."

"How are the new students performing? Is the school doing its job properly?"

"Absolutely. I would put our school up against any in the country."

Pleased by her unmistakable loyalty to the company, Geoff nodded. "Enough about business—let's talk about you."

She gave him a look that warned him she wouldn't fall easily for the usual trite lines, but he hadn't really been feeding her one. He was interested in finding out about her. Something about the contrast between her politely restrained manner and her sexy flame-red dress intrigued him as much as her lovely face and curvy figure attracted him.

It had been much too long since he'd had time to spend an evening with an intriguing woman, he concluded. He had been so busy being the dutiful son and employee during the past ten years that he had almost forgotten how to be spontaneous and impulsive. He had tried so hard to be like his hardworking and upstanding father and not like his wild and irresponsible uncle that he had almost forgotten how to be himself. He had begun to suspect that there was a little of both his father and his uncle inside him.

It was the latter side that he called upon when he leaned slightly forward and gave Cecilia his most winning smile. "What do you like to do when you're not delivering babies?"

"I'm an avid reader and gardener. I enjoy hiking and bird-watching in the mountains."

"How do you feel about football?"

She lifted her wineglass to her lips and studied him over the rim. "I am positively passionate about football. Especially when it comes to University of Kentucky football."

His interest went up a couple more notches. "A woman after my own heart."

"I'm not after anyone's heart, Mr. Bingham," she said, setting her glass on the table. "Hearts are very high-maintenance organs, and I barely have time to take care of myself."

He laughed. Now that was a sentiment he could agree with. With each passing moment he was becoming more pleased that he had followed his impulses and asked Cecilia Mendoza to join him for dinner.

Cecilia had always believed that the nicest pleasures were unexpected ones. Dining with Geoff Bingham definitely fell into that category. He was very good company—articulate, funny, attentive when she spoke. All skills picked up during the course of his job, she was sure, making him an ideal companion for a leisurely meal.

She couldn't help chuckling as she compared this

outing to the last time she had gone out on a dinner date. At Vanessa's urging, she had reluctantly agreed to a blind date set up over the Internet. After all, there were so few available men Cecilia's age in this area, and with her long hours at the clinic, she didn't have many opportunities to meet other singles.

The date had been a dismal failure, a total waste of time on both sides. He hadn't been at all interested in hearing about her work—just the opposite, actually, since he freely admitted that the idea of childbirth "grossed him out." And his description of midnight frog gigging—his favorite sport, apparently— had done the same for her.

"What's so funny?" Geoff asked, looking up from his nearly finished steak.

She hadn't realized she had laughed out loud. "Nothing. I'm just enjoying the meal."

He glanced at her plate and then at his own. "Maybe I should have ordered the trout. My steak's good, but it doesn't make me laugh."

"Let's just say it's been too long since I've been out for a nice meal with a charming companion," she said, reaching for her wineglass. "I've been eating alone entirely too much lately."

Geoff's expression turned wry. "I almost wish I could say the same. I have very few opportunities to spend any time alone. Seems like I rush constantly from one meeting or reception or dinner party to the next. I can't even tell you the last time I had a chance to crash in front of the TV with a pizza for an entire evening."

"You don't enjoy your work?"

"Actually, I do, for the most part. But I think I'm

going to start scheduling a bit more free time in the future.''

She nodded. "Good plan. Spend too many hours working and too few relaxing and you'll end up burned out and suffering from stress-related health problems. I've seen it entirely too many times."

"Maybe you should take your own advice. From what I hear, you're one of the hardest workers in the clinic."

She wondered who had been talking about her to Geoff. His sister, perhaps? While it sounded as though the conversation had been complimentary, it still made her uncomfortable to think about being discussed in her absence. "Yes, well, like you, I've been giving some thought to my personal life lately."

As much as she loved her work, it was no substitute for a family or for the child she wanted so badly.

"You're not planning on leaving the clinic, are you? Mari would have a cow if you even suggested it."

She laughed at his wording, then shook her head. "I'm not leaving the clinic. I love my job. I just need more."

She changed the subject before he could ask what that "more" entailed. "Tell me about your latest trip. I heard you were in Italy." She wondered how he felt knowing he had been the subject of a few discussions, too.

If it bothered him, he didn't let it show. He merely nodded to confirm the rumor. "Milan. I met with some scientists and international venture capitalists about investing funds and expertise into our biomedical research center."

"Did the meetings go well—or can you say?"

"I can't really give any details at the moment, but I can say the family was satisfied with my progress."

Cecilia toyed with a fork-size piece of tender salmon. "Your family seems to be more than satisfied with your work. They always sound so proud when they speak of you."

She noted that his smile was just a bit crooked. "That's what I've been trained for all my life—to make my family proud."

Was that a trace of restlessness she heard in his voice? She doubted that Geoff had been given much choice about joining his family's business. Were there times when he wished he could have pursued his own path?

Cecilia knew all about family obligations. After all, she had pretty much put her own life on hold for several years to care for her mother. She had set aside dating and traveling and experimenting because she felt she owed it to her mother, and because she had wanted to give her much younger brother a chance to finish his education and get started in his own career.

But now their mother was gone. At twenty-six, Eric was successfully established with Bingham Enterprises, blissfully engaged to the woman he adored, and expecting a child he would love with all his heart. Cecilia was thirty-seven and still recovering financially from the daunting medical bills she had hidden from her brother. Her social life was pretty much nonexistent, and having her own child was a dream that seemed farther out of reach with each passing month.

"What's wrong?"

She glanced up from the food she had suddenly lost

interest in to find Geoff watching her from across the table, his clear hazel eyes entirely too perceptive. She felt as if he could read her thoughts in her own brown eyes, and even though she knew that was foolish, she glanced quickly away, pretending to concentrate on her meal again. "Nothing's wrong. Why?"

"You stopped smiling."

She smiled again and tried to make it look completely natural. "No serious talk tonight. I won't allow it. Tell me about Milan—and make me see it in my mind."

Proving himself to be as skilled with words as he was with a smile, he entertained her for the next twenty minutes with stories of his travels. His descriptions were so clever it was almost as if she could see the classic architecture, almost smell the spices and flowers, almost hear the music and voices, almost taste the exotic air. Maybe she would never have a chance to visit Milan for herself, but she would leave this restaurant feeling as if she had been treated to a brief glimpse of the faraway city.

Within minutes her smile was entirely genuine again. And all because of Geoff.

Funny how Geoff had fantasized earlier about spending the evening alone with his guitar. Instead, he found himself doing everything he could think of to delay his return to his empty rooms.

"Are you sure you don't want dessert?" he asked when they could spend no more time toying with their empty plates.

Still wearing the soft smile his word-pictures had evoked, Cecilia shook her head. "I couldn't eat another bite. But feel free to order something for yourself.''

He had no interest in dessert, either. As delectable as the pies here were, they couldn't draw his interest away from the woman across the table from him.

It seemed he was in the mood for spicy rather than sweet this evening.

Somewhat reluctantly he paid the tab and escorted her out of the dining room. The strains of music drifting from the downstairs lounge gave him an idea for prolonging the evening. ''The band sounds good tonight. Unless you're in a hurry to get home, why don't we have a drink and listen for a little while?''

She barely hesitated before agreeing. ''That sounds like fun.''

Immensely pleased with himself, he led her in. Melinda's lounge was a popular weekend date destination, and both the dance floor and the numerous cozy tables were almost full. Geoff thought it was another example of how magical this evening had been so far that a particularly nice table opened up just as they entered.

An efficient waitress took their orders almost as soon as they sat down. Cecilia asked for white wine, and Geoff requested the same.

The band—a group of talented local thirty-somethings—played a mix of adult contemporary and country pop numbers, the most popular genres for the usual crowd here. Geoff tapped his foot in time with a lively rendition of ''Boot Scoot Boogie.'' Energetic dancers two-stepped and line danced on the polished wood floor.

Geoff could two-step with the best of them, but he

was rather hoping a nice, slow number would be next. The thought of holding Cecilia Mendoza in his arms was enough to make his foot tap faster.

She seemed to be enjoying watching the dancers. An amused smile flitted across her lips as she focused on one rhythmically challenged couple in matching turquoise western shirts and ill-fitting jeans.

Taking advantage of the opportunity to watch her without her noticing, he admired the way the flickering candlelight and colored dance floor lights gleamed in her dark hair. Wispy tendrils had escaped her upsweep to sway against her cheeks and flirt with the tops of her shoulders. He would like to see her hair down. Even more, he would like to see it spread across his pillow.

She chose that moment, of course, to glance his way, making him hope his thoughts were well concealed. "The band is good, aren't they?"

"Very good," he agreed, though he hadn't heard a note since he'd started gazing at her.

She leaned a bit closer to him so he could hear her over the music and surrounding conversations. Though he could hear her perfectly well when she made another comment about the music, he scooted his own chair a bit closer to hers when he replied.

She lifted an eyebrow when his knee brushed hers. "You aren't getting fresh, are you, Mr. Bingham?"

He grinned and ran a fingertip slowly down her smooth bare arm. "I was sort of thinking about it."

"Well, let me know when you decide."

"Are you telling me it's okay if I do get fresh?"

She gave him a smile that heated his blood to a

low simmer. "I suppose you'll just have to try it and see."

Obligingly enough, the band slipped into a slow number, the country arrangement of "I Don't Want to Miss a Thing." As of that moment, it was Geoff's new favorite song.

He stood and held out his hand. "Dance with me?"

Though she placed her hand in his and rose obligingly enough, she murmured, "I'm not much of a dancer, I'm afraid."

Somehow he doubted that, considering the graceful way she moved, the gentle sway of her hips. But he couldn't care less about fancy steps or choreographed moves—he just wanted to get his arms around her.

It felt as good to have them there as he had predicted.

Funny that he hadn't realized until now how small she was. He would guess her to be a good seven inches shorter than his own six feet, so that even the strappy, heeled sandals she wore brought the top of her head just to his chin. Her figure was slender but nicely curved, making his hands itch to wander and explore. He kept them discreetly placed for public dancing, but he couldn't help fantasizing a bit….

"It's been forever since I've danced," Cecilia murmured.

"It's been a while for me, too." The double entendre was unintentional—but accurate, nonetheless. When another couple crowded them, bringing Cecilia more closely against him, he was forcefully reminded of just how long it had been since he'd spent any quality one-on-one time with an attractive woman. It took some effort for him to keep his body from embarrassing him like a randy teenager's.

They spent the next hour dancing and talking. Flirting. Having fun. Geoff could almost feel the last traces of work-induced tension seeping from his muscles. He sensed the same thing in Cecilia as her smiles warmed and softened.

It was inevitable that other people there recognized them with apparent surprise and curiosity, but other than acknowledging greetings, Geoff ignored everyone but his companion. Cecilia did the same, exchanging the occasional smile or wave, but subtly discouraging further approaches.

She was good at that, Geoff decided. Politely reserved. It was a skill his late mother had perfected and that Geoff had worked to develop to preserve some semblance of privacy in his hectic and very public life.

Though he paid little attention to gossip, his prominent family having been the subject of all too much of it during the years, he wondered if it bothered Cecilia that they were attracting so much notice. Tongues would probably wag tomorrow about Geoff making time with one of the midwives from the clinic. He was cynical enough to know that a few would turn the question around. ''Didja' hear that Cecilia Mendoza was making a play to snag the Bingham's bachelor son?''

Such idle talk didn't concern him, but maybe Cecilia took it more seriously. Then again, maybe not. After all, she must have known when they agreed to dine here that plenty of people would recognize them and speculate.

He had the feeling that Cecilia was self-confident enough not to be overly concerned at what other people said about her. He admired that about her. It was only one of the things he admired about her, he mused, his gaze lingering on her lush mouth.

Cecilia was reluctant for the evening to end, and it was clear that Geoff felt the same way. She couldn't remember the last time she'd had such a pleasant outing. She certainly couldn't recall the last time she had danced this much. Even if her feet were throbbing in the heeled sandals she hadn't expected to wear this long, it was well worth the discomfort.

It was a heady feeling knowing that Geoff found her attractive. Too often lately she had felt routine-bound and uninteresting, her days consumed with work, her home life unfulfilling. She was so often surrounded by young nurses and young mothers, who often treated Cecilia with a deference usually reserved for much older women. It was a sign of their respect for her and her career, of course, and she acknowledged that. But their attitudes sometimes made her feel older than thirty-seven.

Now a man at least five years her junior was looking at her with desire and admiration in his eyes. A very attractive, successful, interesting and respected man, who must meet dozens of beautiful and fascinating women in his travels.

She didn't expect this to go anywhere, of course. Nor did she particularly want it to. After all, Geoff was a Bingham—and she certainly didn't want to be involved in *their* lives. It concerned her enough that her brother was marrying one of the notorious Binghams—even though Hannah was only loosely connected to the clan.

Still, Cecilia thought, as Geoff's strong arms went around her for their final dance, it had been nice to enjoy his company for a few stolen hours.

He held her more closely this time. His cheek rested against her hair. The band played Lonestar's "Amazed," the lead singer crooning the words into the mike. Whenever she heard the song in the future, she would remember this dance and the deliciously shivery sensations running through her.

Geoff was a skilled dancer who made it very easy for her to follow his lead. A smooth turn brought them even closer together, her breasts brushing against his chest, their thighs touching as their feet moved in unison. She felt a tug of response deep inside her, a dull ache that she acknowledged as pure physical desire. It had been much too long since she had indulged that side of herself.

The song ended eventually. Inevitably. Geoff held her for just a moment after the last note faded away, and then he stepped back. "I suppose we should go," he said as he escorted her back to their table. "It's getting late, and I know you must be tired."

She was a bit tired, actually, and her feet were killing her, but she was tempted to ask him to stay a little while longer. Instead, she merely nodded. "It is getting late."

He stayed close by her side as he walked her out. Cecilia could almost feel eyes watching them leave, and she knew there would be talk tomorrow. She didn't particularly care.

From her early childhood as one of the town's few

residents of Hispanic descent at that time, she had accepted that people thought of her as different. People had talked when her father died in a senseless whitewater-rafting accident when Cecilia was still in elementary school. They had whispered when her mother bore an out-of-wedlock son when Cecilia was eleven. Maria had raised both children on her own because Eric's no-good father hadn't stayed around to help.

Maria had lived quietly, but somewhat defiantly, working as many as three jobs and asking for no help from anyone except Cecilia, who had served almost as surrogate mother to her baby brother. Though she'd had little spare time to devote to her children, Maria's strength and self-sufficiency had set an example for both Cecilia and Eric to pursue their own goals without being overly influenced by anyone else.

The gossip had started again when Cecilia had impulsively married at nineteen, a marriage that had lasted barely two years. Six years her senior, Gary McGhee had swept her off her feet and into his arms, promising her everything she had ever dreamed of— a loving partner, an encouraging supporter, a caring father for the children she had wanted even then. Someone to take care of her, for a change.

She had discovered quickly enough that what he had really wanted was someone strong to take care of *him.* An adoring young wife who wouldn't mind putting her own dreams aside so she could serve as his personal cheerleader while he drifted from one get-rich scheme to another.

She had finally accepted that Gary was all talk and that she had made a mistake to believe any of it. She had come to the decision that she would rather pursue her own goals by herself—like her mother—than to give them up for someone who would never appreciate the sacrifice.

And now people were talking about her family again as her brother prepared to marry a woman who carried another man's baby. A woman who had, herself, been an illegitimate child of notorious bad-boy Billy Bingham.

Knowing how deeply Eric loved Hannah, and what a good father he would make for her child, Cecilia didn't care if the gossips talked until their tongues deflated. It was no one's business but Eric's who he married or why. Just as it was no one else's business if Cecilia wanted to enjoy Geoff Bingham's company for a few delightful hours.

Let them gossip, she thought with a private smile. These memories would be hers to savor for quite some time.

"You're smiling again," Geoff observed, turning at her car door to study her in the yellow glow of the parking lot lights.

"I had a lovely time," she told him, tilting her smile up for him.

"So did I." Ignoring anyone who might see them, he lowered his head and brushed a quick kiss against her cheek. As relatively innocent as the gesture was, it still made her knees go weak to feel his lips against her skin.

Geoff lifted his head, and though he was still smiling, there was a new heat in his eyes. "Sorry. I couldn't resist."

"Did you hear me protest?"

"No." He bent toward her again. "So maybe you wouldn't mind if I—"

She moved quickly out of his reach. A disregard for gossip was one thing, but her deeply entrenched sense of privacy prevented her from making a complete spectacle of herself. "This is a little too public for my taste."

He pushed his hands into his pockets as if to demonstrate that he wouldn't touch her again without permission. "Would you allow me to see you home? Just to make sure you get there safely?"

Though she wasn't sure her safety had much to do with the offer, she took a moment to think about it. She supposed there was no harm in allowing him to follow her home. The fifteen-minute drive would give him the satisfaction of making a chivalrous gesture— and her the chance to think about whether she wanted to invite him inside when they got there.

She simply nodded and turned to slide into her car.

By the time she drove into her driveway, she had conducted a full, somewhat heated debate with herself about how she wanted the evening to end. Should she politely thank Geoff again for dinner, then send him on his way? Or should she ask him in for a nightcap and then see what happened?

Just how far was she willing to suspend reality this evening?

Chapter Three

Geoff parked his expensive, new-looking sports car behind the economy sedan Cecilia had bought used four years ago—another sign, she mused, that their lives couldn't be more different. And then he moved toward her, his face shadowed, his lean, strong, yet somehow elegant body silhouetted by security lighting.

Even the way he walked fascinated her, she thought as she watched him approach. He held his head high and his shoulders squared—an innate air of confidence that probably came with being born a Bingham. It wasn't arrogance she sensed in him, exactly—more an expectation of being accepted and respected, a feeling that had been lacking in her own background.

This man could have spent the evening anywhere he wanted—and with anyone—but he had chosen to spend it with her. She couldn't deny that it was a huge boost to her feminine ego.

He stopped in front of her. "Nice neighborhood."

"Thank you. I enjoy living here."

It was an older neighborhood, filled with aging houses—and aging residents, many of whom had lived here since Cecilia was a little girl. The teenage girl next door was the youngest resident of the neighborhood since moving in with her grandparents a year ago.

Tall, stately trees guarded the sides of the narrow street, their branches nearly touching over it. Neat yards and flourishing flower beds gave testament to the pride her working-class neighbors took in their homes.

Cecilia had inherited her small white-frame house when her mother passed away three years earlier. Though she had protested, Eric had insisted on signing his half over to her—in gratitude, he had said, for her putting her own life on hold to care for their mother while he completed his education and embarked on his career.

Cecilia's name was the only one on the deed now, but she still considered it Eric's home, too. He made a point of keeping up the routine maintenance for her—such as painting the siding and shutters and flower boxes last spring—and he ate lunch with her every Sunday.

At least, he had until very recently, she corrected herself with a little ripple of sadness. Now that Eric was about to be married and was establishing his own family, some of the old routines had to change, Sunday lunches being one of them. As much as she welcomed Hannah into the family, Cecilia couldn't help regretting a little that her role as the most important woman in Eric's life had come to an end.

Now she wasn't the most important person in anyone's life, she had found herself thinking during the middle of several long, lonely nights. Though she had never been the type to indulge in self-pity, she was human enough to wish some things had turned out differently for her.

"Have you lived here long?"

Pulling herself back to the present, she replied to Geoff, "Since I was very young. This is the house where my mother raised Eric and me."

Geoff nodded, his face still obscured by the shadows of the warm summer night. "You must miss her very much."

"Yes, I do."

"I miss my mom, too."

The simple and palpably sincere statement brought a lump to her throat. She remembered Geoff's mother—a beautiful, classy, kind-hearted woman who had been known as a tireless contributor to local charities. At only forty, Violet Bingham had died of a massive heart attack. That was almost ten years ago. Cecilia had been a relatively new employee of the clinic, but even then she had seen how the tragedy had devastated the family and the community.

People who knew him well said that Geoff's father, Ron, would never get over the loss of his young wife. Cecilia had always considered it a shame that handsome, charming, still-vibrant Ronald Bingham should spend the rest of his life alone.

Maybe it was the moment of bonding or maybe it

was the thought of the empty rooms waiting for her that made her say, "Would you like to come in for coffee? Or if you're too tired, I—"

"I would love to come in for coffee," he agreed before she could even finish the sentence. "I'll just go lock my car first."

Hoping she wasn't making a gigantic mistake, Cecilia turned toward her front door.

Trying to be subtle about it, Geoff studied Cecilia's home curiously when he followed her inside. The love of bright colors revealed by the red dress she had worn this evening was echoed in the decor of her living room. The sofa looked new—a splash of bright graphics on a deep-red background. The few wood pieces were old—a mix of refinished and fashionably distressed antiques.

On the walls hung framed prints of impressionistic paintings. The jewel-toned throw pillows scattered about the furniture had probably been hand crafted. It was a room that had been decorated by someone with excellent taste and limited funds. He liked it better than many expensive and professionally decorated rooms he had been in.

He made note of the framed photographs grouped on the mantel. Most of them were of Eric, from infancy through adulthood. Eric lying on a bear rug, blowing out three candles on a birthday cake, posing in Boy Scout and baseball uniforms, beaming in cap and gown. A dark-eyed brunette who could only be Cecilia's mother appeared in a few of the photos, looking stiff and camera-shy. Cecilia was pictured

even less, either because she didn't like being pho-
tographed or didn't care to display pictures of herself.

It was obvious that she adored her younger brother.
Geoff was quite sure that his own sister had no similar
photographic shrine to *him*. He and Mari had always
gotten along well enough, though they had been too
busy and focused on their careers to connect much
during the past decade. Since their mother's death,
actually.

Violet had been the glue that held her family together. Their grief over her loss had caused them to
drift apart, throwing themselves more fully into their
activities to dull the pain.

Cecilia motioned toward the couch. "Have a seat.
I'll put the coffee on."

He placed a hand on her arm. "I have a confession
to make."

Her eyebrows lifted in question. "What?"

"I don't really want any coffee."

She tilted her head to study his face, her expression
hard to interpret. "Is that right?"

"I don't even like coffee."

"So you came in because…?"

"Because I wasn't ready for the evening to be
over."

The admission certainly didn't seem to surprise her.
Nor did it appear to perturb her. She had to have
known when he'd followed her home that the moment
would come when she would have to decide how she
wanted their evening to end.

Maybe she had made that decision when she invited him in. She glanced at his hand where it rested
on her arm and then looked back up at him through

her thick, dark lashes. The smile that played on her lips was neither shy nor hesitant, but the smile of a woman who knew what she wanted. And tonight, it seemed, she wanted him.

"Then maybe we can make it last just a little while longer," she murmured, sliding her free hand up his chest.

His pulse rate sped up in anticipation. "Just for a little while," she had said, making it clear that she wasn't expecting more from him than this one night. She was no starry-eyed ingenue who would take his attentions too seriously. No hungry, wannabe socialite hoping to secure a country-club future by snagging a most-eligible bachelor.

Perhaps that was why he'd had such a good time with her tonight. She'd had no expectations, no demands of him. He hadn't been trying to sell her anything or charm anything out of her, and the same had been true in reverse. He had been free to be himself— to eat what he'd liked, to talk without overanalyzing his words, to laugh and dance and sometimes sit quietly and listen to the music.

Damn, it had felt good. He wanted to hang on to that feeling for a bit longer. He released her arm only to slide both of his own around her. "I suppose you've been told that you have beautiful eyes."

She gave him a look that was a mixture of amusement and reproach. "You've been refreshingly natural all evening. Don't start spouting corny lines now."

He laughed, though it hadn't really been a line. She *did* have beautiful eyes. And an absolutely amazing mouth. And a body that seemed to have been tailored to fit nicely against his.

"Okay," he promised. "No corny lines."

She seemed to give that vow a moment's thought, and then she shook her head and slid her arms around his neck. "Oh, the heck with it. Tell me more about my eyes."

He was still grinning when he covered her mouth with his.

He had been fantasizing all evening about tasting her full, soft lips. He discovered now that imagination couldn't compare to reality when it came to kissing Cecilia Mendoza.

Though he had bent down to her, she stood on tiptoe to meet him. The position brought her even more snugly against him, making him intensely aware of the womanly fullness of her breasts and hips. Geoff had always appreciated curves, having never been a fan of the fashionably underfed look.

He no longer tried to hide the effect she had on him. They weren't in public now, and he felt free to be completely honest with her. If she didn't know how much he wanted her by now, then she simply wasn't paying attention.

He surfaced from the kiss long enough for them both to draw quick breaths of air, and then he dove in again. As waves of pleasure swept through him, he found himself thinking about how glad he was that he had changed his mind about spending the evening alone with his guitar.

No woman should reach the age of forty without having at least a few reckless adventures to remember, Cecilia figured. And since she was getting rather close to that particular milestone, this was one adventure she simply could not resist.

Kissing Geoff was a revelation. Who would have thought any man could make her feel so much with no more than a couple of deep, skillful kisses? She was typically a bit slower off the mark, so to speak. But then, it had been quite a long time since she had participated in the sport.

She could feel the heat in her face when he finally drew back. Her hair was beginning to slip its restraints, lying against her cheeks and tickling the nape of her neck. She knew she must look flushed and disheveled, but still Geoff gazed at her as though he found her beautiful. And while she knew she wasn't, really, it still felt nice to have him look at her that way.

His smile was crooked, and his voice satisfyingly gravelly when he said, "I should warn you that I feel another corny line coming on."

She cleared her throat. "I'm getting close to spouting a few myself."

"As much as I would like to hear any outrageous compliments you choose to make about me, maybe it would be better if we move the conversation to another location. We could at least sit down. Or, if it's getting too late, you could walk me to the door...."

Another gentlemanly way to offer her an out if she had any doubts. He really was a nice guy, Cecilia thought as she slid her fingers into the back of his neatly brushed hair. She couldn't help thinking how nice it would look tousled around his handsome face.

Because he held her so tightly against him, she knew their kisses had affected him as deeply as they had her. Yet his lightly spoken words had been intended to ease any tension their passionate kisses might have created between them. Geoff wanted her to feel comfortable with him, the way she had at the restaurant earlier. He was obviously trying to reassure her that he was putting no pressure on her, that she was fully in control.

While she appreciated his consideration, she almost wished he would sweep her off her feet so she didn't have to make any decisions. It was an uncharacteristic thought, and one she quickly suppressed, since she was admittedly a control freak who wanted the final say in all areas of her life.

"Maybe you would like to see the rest of my house," she said, giving him a smile designed to let him know exactly what the invitation included.

"There's nothing I would like more," he assured her huskily.

She took his hand. His fingers closed eagerly around hers.

Because there was no way she could have known anyone would be joining her in her bedroom that evening, it must have been a lucky impulse that had made Cecilia change her sheets and put out fresh flowers from her garden before she left for work that morning. She enjoyed coming home to a clean house after a long day in the clinic, and tonight the faint whiff of the flowers only added to the romantic haze she had slipped into.

The small Tiffany-style lamp on her nightstand was connected to a timer so she didn't have to walk into a dark room after working late. The lamp glowed softly now, throwing gentle illumination over the 1930s-era dark pecan bedroom furniture and the hand-pieced quilt she used as a bedspread. Period accessories gleaned from flea markets and antique shops decorated the vanity and double dresser, and more family photos hung on the walls. Numerous soft, colorful throw pillows turned the room into an old-fashioned, comfy boudoir, complete with a bentwood rocker tucked into one corner.

This was Cecilia's haven, the place where she hid out to read and daydream. Though the decor had changed, it was the same room she'd had as a girl, never having the desire to move into the rooms that had been used by her mother or her brother. She rarely brought anyone in; even Eric had stepped foot in her room only a handful of times, and then only to make various repairs.

It took an enormous leap of faith for her to invite Geoff Bingham into her private space. For a woman who generally took as few risks as possible in her life, this was pretty huge on the adventure scale.

Maybe he sensed her sudden attack of nerves. He turned to her and gave her a smile that was both gentle and endearing. "It's not too late to walk me to the door."

"I know, but the thing is, I don't want to do that yet."

"Can't say it's what I want you to do, either," he murmured, his smile crooked again.

Drawing a deep breath, she walked her fingers up his chest. "Tell me again about my eyes."

"They are—" he lowered his head to speak against her lips "—amazing."

She let herself drift into the kiss, into the moment. She'd had a few great kisses in her life—some that she would have described at the time as spectacular— but there was something different about kissing Geoff. She couldn't think of a word that wasn't clichéd or trite or simply inadequate, but there was definitely something....

Apparently he found time to work out during his travels. Beneath the conservative businessman's clothing was a lean, solid, nicely muscled body. She had noticed that during their first slow dance. Her observation was confirmed when she slid his jacket off his shoulders and tossed it over the rocker. Even through his shirt, she could see that his shoulders were wide and his stomach flat. What she *couldn't* see, she mused as she went to work on his tie, was whether his chest was smooth or furry. Tanned or pale.

Only moments later she was able to confirm that he was lightly tanned and that there was only a smattering of dark hair down the center of his chest. Drawing his shirt slowly down his arms, she tried to anticipate how it would feel to be pressed against that very nice chest, with nothing between them except desire.

She couldn't wait to find out.

Holding her gaze with his own, he slipped his hands behind her. A brush of cool air followed her zipper down her back, and then her dress pooled around her bare feet. She couldn't really remember kicking off her sandals, but then the details of this night were beginning to blur into a haze of sensation. She had given up on rational thought a long time ago—maybe even the first time Geoff had smiled at her.

Unfortunately, her intuition hadn't warned her to don sexy lingerie beneath the red dress. She was still wearing the serviceable beige bra and matching panties she had worn to work. Before she had time to regret the choice, the problem had become moot; Cecilia barely had time to reflect on how suspiciously good Geoff was at removing women's undergarments before she found herself in his arms again. With nothing between them but desire.

It felt even better than she could have imagined.

As he lowered her to the bed, she came very close to telling him that she never did things like this. That it was so unlike her to bring a man she had just met into her bed. She bit the words back because they sounded so overused. So difficult to believe—even though in this case they were so absolutely true.

She could only hope he somehow understood without being told that this was a special evening. A brief visit to fantasyland.

Reality intruded momentarily when he retrieved a plastic package from his pants pocket—did he *always* carry condoms or had he hoped to hook up with someone tonight?—but she pushed the question to the back of her mind to ponder later.

He kissed her eyelids. "Have I mentioned that I have a thing for big brown eyes?"

"I—" She was forced to clear her throat before she could speak. Apparently the fact that they were practically glued together in her bed wasn't affecting his voice the way it was hers, though it was certainly affecting other parts of him dramatically enough. "I think you have."

His lips trailed across her cheek. "Did I tell you how much I like the dimples at the corners of your mouth?" he asked, then pressed a kiss just there.

She felt those dimples deepen. "I don't think you have mentioned that."

The tip of his tongue swept across her lower lip, causing a shiver of reaction. "Consider it said."

She could only nod this time.

Scooting downward a bit on the bed, he nibbled a line from her chin down her throat to the top of her shoulder. "Should I keep listing the parts of you that I like best? Because I warn you, it could take the rest of the night."

Arching into his explorations, she closed her eyes and threaded her fingers into his hair. "I just happen to be available all night," she managed to say.

He lifted his head from his downward path just long enough to flash her a wickedly beautiful smile. "I can't tell you how glad I am to hear that."

The outrageous idea came to her while she was making coffee the next morning. It hit her with enough force to make her stumble, almost dumping coffee grounds on the spotless linoleum floor.

She placed a hand on a countertop to steady her while she took a moment to wonder if she had just slipped over the edge of sanity. Surely she must be crazy to even consider what she suddenly found herself contemplating.

Dimly aware of the sound of the shower running in the back of the house, she knew she had only a few minutes to gather her composure—and, perhaps, her courage—before facing Geoff.

It was still early on this Saturday morning—not quite 8 a.m. She'd woken first, a bit startled with the realization that she wasn't alone in her bed. Resisting the opportunity to watch Geoff sleep—and he had looked as delicious with tousled hair and a shadow of beard as she had thought he would—she had slipped out of the bed and into the shower.

By the time Geoff had roused, looking a bit embarrassed that jet lag and a strenuous night had caused him to sleep so heavily, Cecilia had already donned a T-shirt and shorts, pulled her hair into a loose braid and applied judicious touches of makeup. Urging him to take his time in the shower, she had promised to have breakfast ready when he came out.

Hastily dumping coffee into the filter, she turned on the coffeemaker and set out cereal, fruit, milk and yogurt on the kitchen table. Remembering Geoff's choice of steak and potato for dinner last night, she wouldn't be surprised if he preferred a bacon-and-eggs breakfast, but this was what she had on hand.

She should probably wait until after they had eaten before broaching the proposition that had hit her with such staggering force. He would need the energy, she thought wryly, when he bolted in panic from the crazy woman he had awakened with this morning. Could she really expect him to react any other way?

But did she have any logical choice but to ask him? How else would she know if it was even within the realm of possibility?

Geoff came into the kitchen then, and her heart tripped—whether from nerves or a surge of raw attraction, she couldn't have said. Probably both. He looked younger, somehow, with his hair still damp and his white shirt open at the collar and rolled up on his arms. He hadn't shaved, and the scruffiness only added to that sexy-young-rebel look that was so deceptive for the button-down businessman she suspected him to be.

She swallowed and rubbed her palms on her khaki shorts, suddenly feeling every day of the five years she had on him. Though she didn't usually have issues with vanity—no more than any other woman, anyway—she found herself hoping those extra years weren't immediately visible.

Geoff smiled, only adding to his extraordinary appeal. He brushed a light kiss across her mouth. "Looks good."

"I hope you like fruit and cereal."

He chuckled as he glanced at the table. "Oh, yeah. The food looks good, too."

A silly blush warmed her cheeks. Heaven only knew when she had last blushed that way, she thought with a shake of her head. She had to get herself under control. If a simple flirtatious compliment turned her into a giggling schoolgirl, how could she begin to talk to him about certain much more serious—yet undeniably awkward—matters?

"Sit down. I'll pour the coffee," she said, turning toward the coffeemaker. And then she stopped and whacked her forehead with the palm of her hand. "Oh, darn. I forgot. You don't drink coffee."

He laughed and patted her shoulder on his way to the table. "No. But feel free to have some yourself."

"I drink too much coffee, anyway. It's my one

vice.'' And because that sounded like such a foolish statement after last night, she blushed again.

She tried to hide it by turning her back to him and opening the refrigerator door. ''I have juice. Apple or grape. Eric loves fruit juices, so I try to keep plenty on hand.''

Stop babbling, Cecilia. She really did have to get a stronger grip on her emotions this morning.

''Apple juice sounds good. Thanks.''

They finally settled at the table—she with her coffee, he with a glass of apple juice.

''Looks like it's going to be a nice day,'' Geoff remarked, nodding toward the window over the sink. His light tone indicated that he was trying to start a casual conversation. Maybe he sensed that she was tense this morning. If so, he probably attributed it to morning-after jitters, maybe after-the-fact misgivings.

He had no clue, of course, what was really making her so nervous. If he did, he couldn't have looked so calm.

Trying to put on a show of being completely relaxed, she responded to his comments in kind and toyed with her breakfast, making a pretense of enjoying it. Actually, her throat was so tight she thought she might choke if she tried to eat much.

When he had finished his meal, Geoff pushed his plate aside and laced his hands on the table. ''Okay,'' he said, leveling a look at her. ''What's wrong? Second thoughts about last night? Regrets?''

''No. As uncharacteristic as it was for me, I don't regret anything that happened last night.''

His smile turned gentle. ''I never doubted that the night was hardly routine for you.''

And now she worried that he was misinterpreting her admission that she wasn't exactly a party girl. "It isn't as if I'm making too big a deal out of what happened between us last night," she assured him hastily. "I mean, I am a thirty-seven-year-old divorcee."

He reached out to cover her hand with his. "It *was* a big deal, Cecilia. One of the best nights I've had in a very long time."

She laced her fingers with his. "For me, too."

"So what's the problem?"

"I'm sort of afraid of ruining everything now."

"Not possible."

"You haven't heard what I want to ask you yet."

Though she saw a touch of wariness enter his eyes—poor guy, she couldn't blame him, considering how awkwardly she was handling this—he managed to keep his expression politely encouraging. "What do you want to ask?"

She drew her hand from his and reached for her coffee cup, relieved to see that it was steady when she lifted it to her lips. After a bracing sip, she began, "I'm thirty-seven years old."

"Yes, so you said."

"I was married once. A long time ago. It didn't work out."

"You mentioned that, too." He sipped his juice, eyeing her curiously over the rim of his glass.

She was really making a hash of this. Clearing her throat, she tried again. "The thing is, I've never had an overwhelming urge to remarry. I love my home and my work and I would rather be contentedly single than unhappily married."

"We agree on that point. My family's been nagging me to marry for years, but to be honest, I simply have no desire to do so at this point. I just don't want to be responsible for anyone else's happiness and welfare." He still looked a bit wary as he clearly spelled out his position.

Realizing the direction his thoughts were taking, she laughed a little and held up her hands. "Relax, Geoff. I'm not asking you to marry me. As pleasant as our night together was, it hasn't turned me into a starry-eyed romantic with foolish dreams of happily ever after."

Though he looked marginally relieved, he seemed contradictorily perturbed with her choice of adjectives. "Pleasant?"

"*Very* pleasant," she clarified a bit impatiently. She had almost forgotten to make allowances for the male ego during this impromptu proposition.

"So what is this request you have of me?"

She drew a deep breath, then blurted the words before she lost her nerve. "I want you to help me make a baby."

Chapter Four

Geoff wondered for a moment if an unexpected night of passion had somehow damaged his hearing. Surely Cecilia hadn't just said what he thought she had said. "You want me to do *what?*"

He watched as she moistened her lips with the tip of her tongue, a gesture that seemed uncharacteristically nervous from this woman who had appeared so self-confident and composed the night before.

"I want a child," she repeated. "I want to be a mother. And since my prospects of that are getting slimmer as time passes, I'm ready to do whatever is necessary to make that dream come true for me."

She locked her slender, capable hands on the table in front of her as she spoke, her gleaming white knuckles giving further evidence of the tension she was trying not to show.

Geoff shook his head. Wasn't this his luck? He had been telling himself that last night had been a rare gift—unplanned, uncalculated, uncomplicated. A brief foray into the wild side for wild Billy Bingham's straitlaced and compulsively responsible nephew. And now it turned out that the woman he thought he'd charmed into bed had her own reasons for ending up there.

"You're looking at me as though I've grown another head," Cecilia said ruefully. "I know this has taken you by surprise."

"You could say that again."

Her fingers twisted even more tightly. "The thing is, this subject has been on my mind a lot lately. Every day I deliver other women's babies, and every day I wonder whether I'll ever have one of my own. I would be a good mother. I'm mature and responsible and patient. I practically raised Eric, since my mother worked all the time, so I know what I would be getting into. The preschool day-care center at the clinic would give me a chance to see my child often during the day. I'm ready physically, emotionally and financially—as much as I can be, anyway. I don't want to waste any more time."

"So have you, um, thought about adoption?" he asked, still trying to assimilate what she wanted of him.

"I've considered adoption, but it's still rather difficult for a single working woman to be approved, and private adoptions can be terribly expensive. Besides, I would really love to have a child of my own. The artificial insemination process is, again, so expensive that it would be hard for me to afford it. The best option for me seems to be the old-fashioned method.''

''With me.'' It sounded so improbable when he said it that he couldn't help wondering again if he had completely misinterpreted her request.

Her cheeks were a bit pink, but she held her head high. ''It occurred to me this morning that it wouldn't hurt to ask you. After all, we got along very well last night, and we've already taken the biggest step.''

His frown deepened. ''I used protection last night.''

''Yes, I know. Um, do you always carry a couple of packets with you?''

Now it was his turn to be self-conscious. ''I got them out of my car. After you invited me in. Just in case we—''

Hell, this conversation wasn't about defending *his* motives. ''So when you asked me in last night, you were planning to—''

''No!'' Her eyes wide, she cut him off sharply. ''I didn't plan anything that happened last night. I thought I would make an appearance at the reception and then come home—alone—for a grilled cheese sandwich and an evening with a mystery novel. When you asked me to dinner, I expected a nice meal and then a polite good-evening in the parking lot. And when I invited you in, it was an impulse, based on the lovely time we'd had at Miranda's. You said you didn't want the evening to end—and I didn't, either.''

He couldn't help being skeptical, despite the ring of sincerity in her voice. Having been raised in a wealthy and influential family, he had learned long ago that all too many people had hidden motives when it came to their dealings with him.

She began to frown, as if his thoughts had been apparent to her. "I'm really making a mess of this, and I apologize for that. I know it seems outrageous of me to even suggest something like this after knowing you such a short time. As I said, it's something I've been considering, and when this opportunity popped up—well, it just seemed like I would be foolish not to at least ask if you would consider helping me out."

He stood and walked to the coffeemaker, where he slipped a mug off the nearby holder and filled it to the brim with the dark, hot brew.

"I thought you didn't like coffee."

"I seem to need the caffeine jolt. I'm having a little trouble thinking clearly this morning. And, besides, it's too early for scotch."

She waited until he had returned to his seat and had taken a bracing sip of the coffee—which wasn't bad, considering—before she spoke again. "You probably think I have ulterior motives in making this request of you. That's a natural assumption, of course. I should have expected—anyway, I know a man with your connections has to be careful. I want to assure you that I've been entirely straightforward about my goals.

"I want a child, but that's all. I would be willing to sign anything you draw up waiving any claim to money from you for any reason. I am fully prepared to support my child both financially and emotionally. I can't say the child will be raised with a lot of extra money, but I can provide all the necessities and an occasional luxury without any help from anyone else.

To be honest, I prefer it that way at this stage in my life.''

He set his coffee mug on the table with a thud. ''So, basically, what you want is for me to create a baby with you, then simply go away and leave you alone to raise the kid with no input from me.''

She shifted restlessly in her chair. ''You make it sound rather cold when you put it that way.''

''You think?'' He knew he sounded curt, but what could she expect after blindsiding him this way?

Looking defensive, Cecilia glared across the table at him. ''You needn't make it sound as though I've insulted you by asking you to be the father of my child.''

''Maybe I think you have.''

''Just the opposite, I would say. You're intelligent, attractive, healthy—all qualities I would be pleased for my child to inherit.''

''And yet you think I'm the kind of man who would make a child and then walk away from it without a backward glance.''

''It isn't as if there aren't plenty of other illegitimate Binghams living in Merlyn County,'' she shot back.

Geoff watched through narrowed eyes as Cecilia's face paled in response to the echo of her own words, then went bright pink. ''None of those children are mine,'' he said after letting her squirm for a few long moments.

''I'm sorry,'' she said stiffly. Placing both hands flat on the table, she pushed herself to her feet. ''This was obviously a huge mistake. Please forget I said anything. And don't feel obligated to call me again after you leave, not even for courtesy's sake. Let's just pretend our date ended before breakfast.''

He rose more slowly, keeping his eyes on her face, which she was doing her best to hide behind a silky curtain of dark hair. "So you've changed your mind about trying to have a child?"

"I didn't say that. I'm just going to have to explore other options."

Other options being another man to father the baby she apparently wanted so desperately that she'd been willing to risk this embarrassment with him, he realized abruptly. And it said something about his state of mind that thinking of her approaching another man—any other man—with her offer bothered him almost as badly as the fact that she had thought he would go along with her scheme.

"Look, Cecilia, I can tell how important this is to you. Maybe there's something I can do to help. I mean, you work in a place that specializes in fertility treatments. Sure, artificial insemination can get expensive, especially if it takes a few times to produce results, but I'm sure something can be worked out. Installment payments, maybe. Or a bank loan. In fact, I can—"

"No!" She tossed her hair back to give him a glittering look. "No," she repeated more quietly. "Thank you. I can handle this."

Which meant another man again, he thought with a scowl.

"This is really getting awkward. Please, Geoff, just forget it. Actually, I have a lot of things to do today, and I wouldn't want to keep you away from the things I'm sure you have to do. Besides, my brother pops in

sometimes on weekends to help with a few maintenance chores, and it would be very uncomfortable for
me if he were to find you here.''

In other words, here's your hat.

Hustling him out the door, she babbled nervously
the whole time about what a lovely evening she'd
had, and how much she had enjoyed getting to know
him and maybe they would see each other in passing
at the hospital sometime. Unspoken was the addition,
''But not if I see you first.''

Moments later Geoff stood on her front stoop staring blankly at the door that had just been firmly
closed in his face. It appeared his impromptu date
with Cecilia Mendoza had just come to an abrupt,
strange and seemingly permanent end.

All in all, it had been one of the more humiliating
episodes of Cecilia's life. No wonder Geoff had
looked at her as if she had lost her mind. She must
have sounded like an idiot.

She should have expected him to react as he had.
Undoubtedly he now thought of her as a desperate,
aging woman looking to secure a comfortable retire-
ment by duping a wealthy young man into fathering
her child. He probably hadn't believed her for a moment when she'd said she wanted nothing more from
him.

To top it off, she had inadvertently insulted him by
comparing him to his notoriously womanizing grandfather and uncle, even though all the talk she had ever
heard about the Binghams indicated that Geoff and
his father were both complete straight-arrows.

If she were absolutely honest, she would have to

admit that she rather admired Geoff for his instinctive reaction to that comparison. She had become so cynical about men that she had automatically assumed it wouldn't particularly bother him to have no part in an illegitimate child's life.

That was certainly the way his elder relatives had behaved. Rumor had it that Gerald and Billy Bingham had fathered kids all across the county without staying around to be responsible for them. She knew of at least four of Billy Bingham's offspring, her future sister-in-law among them, and Billy hadn't bothered to marry any of the mothers or to be directly involved in his children's lives.

The men in her own family certainly hadn't set any higher example. Eric's father hadn't stayed around to help raise his son. In fact, Reuben had shown no interest in his child at all. He had left before Eric was born and had never made any effort to get back in touch.

Her own father had loved his child, but had continued to pursue his daredevil sports until he'd gotten himself killed. Only within the last few years had Cecilia acknowledged the grief-stricken anger at him that she had carried since. A resentment she was sure her mother had shared, though they had never spoken of it.

As for the man Cecilia had married, it had turned out that he didn't really want children at all, despite what he'd said to the contrary. A child would have interfered with his own immature need to always be the center of attention.

So maybe Geoff was different from so many of the other men Cecilia had known. He had made it apparent that he wasn't interested in being married right now, but she thought he'd also made it clear that if and when he had children, he intended to do so the traditional way. It would certainly be expected of him by his family—and hadn't he told her that he always did what his family expected of him?

She sighed. Oh, well, it hadn't hurt to ask. She would never hear from him again, of course, but she hadn't expected that, anyway. She would spend the rest of the weekend cleaning her house, doing some reading—and giving serious consideration to her plans for motherhood.

Maybe Geoff had given her an idea, after all. Maybe she could swing a loan, mortgage the house, perhaps, to finance fertility treatments. It was definitely a possibility.

She wasn't sure she could ever get up her nerve to make that embarrassing proposition to another man— not that she knew any other reasonable prospects at the moment, anyway.

Too bad about Geoff, though, she thought with another long, regretful sigh.

Geoff sat on his sofa with his guitar across his lap and stared down at the strings, wondering why he had suddenly forgotten how to play. He'd been turning to the guitar in times of stress since he was fourteen, taking pleasure in old Beatles tunes that had been written before he was born. Songs his mother had loved.

Today he couldn't even remember the tunes. His mind was still filled with the echo of Cecilia's voice as she had asked him to father her child.

Despite all the suspicions that had poured through his mind—all the precautions that had been programmed into him almost from birth—he had finally come to the conclusion that she had been completely honest with him. She'd wanted nothing more than what she had asked of him. He simply couldn't believe anything else of her.

She wanted a baby. He supposed he could understand that. Most women did seem to want children, and he imagined Cecilia's biological clock was clamoring pretty loudly at this point. But did she really think he was the kind of man who could walk away from his own kid? A man like—

Like his uncle Billy.

Grimacing, he set the guitar aside and stood to pace. How many times during his late teens and early twenties had he secretly wished he could be more like his father's wild and footloose brother? While Geoff had been bound by smothering rules and regulations, spending his weeknights studying and his weekends working in the family businesses to "build his character," Uncle Billy had been bouncing from one party to another, one beautiful woman to the next.

Billy had tried occasionally to draw his nephew into the fun, urging Geoff to rebel occasionally, to slip away and forget about family expectations, at least temporarily. But, as much as he might have been privately tempted, Geoff had been too tightly bound by the sense of obligation that had been impressed upon him from birth.

He had done everything that was asked of him— and more—without complaint, watching his uncle's exploits with a vague wistfulness. When Billy died piloting one of his expensive airplanes, the family had sadly pointed out how wise Geoff was not to have been influenced by his uncle's wild ways. Hadn't they always predicted that Billy would come to a bad end? While Geoff had taken their lessons to heart, he had grieved for the man who had always been the happy clown among the somber, respectable Binghams.

While his beloved mother had lived, he'd have cut off his arms before he caused her any disappointment or distress. After her death, he'd felt he owed it to his father and sister to cause them no more worry or grief. He had rebelled in only two relatively minor ways since: the big motorcycle he kept in the condo garage, to the great disapproval of both his father and his grandmother; and his refusal to go along with their efforts at finding him a suitable match.

He thought again of the longing look in Cecilia's eyes when she had spoken of the child she wanted so badly. He wished there was something he could do to help her. His awkward offer of financial assistance certainly hadn't impressed her.

It wasn't hard to guess what his uncle would have done. Billy would have happily provided his services in Cecilia's bed until her objective was accomplished, and then he would have moved on to the next adventure without a backward glance.

He knew what his father would say about Cecilia's request. Ron would accuse Geoff of making an error in judgment getting intimately involved with a clinic employee in the first place, even for one night. After another lecture about the expectations of upholding the Bingham name, Ron would remind him about the number of people who would take advantage of him.

He would question the motives of a woman of limited financial means who just happened to choose a man with money to sire her child. And he would predict disaster if Geoff were foolish enough to fall for her scheme.

Was there any way he could combine Billy's daring and Ron's caution and still find a way to help out a new friend?

Cecilia was digging weeds out of the herb garden in her tiny backyard when she heard someone call her name. She swiped the back of one dirty hand across her perspiration-beaded forehead and twisted to look over her shoulder.

"Oh, hi, Brandy," she said to the teenager standing on the other side of the low wooden fence that separated Cecilia's yard from the one next door. "How's it going?"

"Okay. Can I come over?"

"Sure." Cecilia rose, grimacing when her leg and back muscles protested being in a kneeling position for too long. Apparently she had needed a break anyway. "Want some lemonade?"

"Sounds good."

"I'll get us some. We can drink it out here."

Brandy was waiting for her when she came back outside carrying a tray that held two plastic tumblers of lemonade and a plate of oatmeal-raisin cookies. The sixteen-year-old redhead sat in one of the four wrought-iron spring chairs grouped around a small round wrought-iron table. The stone patio on which the furniture was arranged was surrounded by plantings and potted plants and shaded by several large old trees.

Eric had built that little patio for her a couple of years ago, and they had both enjoyed it since. She often ate outside on pretty days.

After handing Brandy her lemonade, Cecilia settled into one of the spring chairs, looking around in satisfaction. There were so many things she liked about her little house, and this tidy backyard was one of her favorite features. It had been a wonderful place to play as a child, to daydream and swing during the daytime, and to gaze at the stars at night.

"Your yard looks good," Brandy said, her gaze following Cecilia's.

"Thank you." Turning her attention back to her guest, Cecilia suddenly frowned. "What happened to your face?"

Brandy shrugged, and one strap of her pink tank top fell off her skinny shoulder. Her shaggy red hair tumbled into her face, which was why Cecilia hadn't immediately noticed the purple bruise that darkened the girl's left cheek. The smattering of acne that marked the girl's skin looked even less attractive in combination with the bruise.

Brandy's green-gold eyes shifted, and she appeared to study the plate of cookies very closely before making her selection. "Played a game of catch and didn't get my glove up fast enough. Caught the ball with my face."

"Ouch. That must have hurt."

"Nah. No big deal. Who was that guy who was here this morning?"

Cecilia swallowed. "Um...guy?" she parroted, stalling for a moment.

"Yeah. I heard a car door and I looked out my window and I saw him drive away in that totally sweet car. It wasn't your brother, was it? He didn't get a new car?"

"No," Cecilia admitted. "He's a man I know through my work."

It was true enough, and all she intended to say to a curious sixteen-year-old. "I haven't seen you around much during the past few weeks. Busy summer?"

"Yeah, kind of. What with my job at South Junction Burgers and my boyfriend and all."

Ah, yes. The boyfriend. Cecilia had seen him a time or two with Brandy, and she hadn't been particularly impressed by the swaggering, wannabe tough guy. From a few brief conversations, she knew Brandy's grandmother worried about the intensity of the relationship, but Maxine Campbell was still being rather hesitant in setting boundaries for the girl.

Another example of a child whose father hadn't bothered to hang around, Brandy had moved in with her grandparents a year ago when her mother's substance abuse had become a problem that could no longer be ignored. Cecilia had befriended the girl then, and she genuinely liked Brandy, but she knew there had been some adolescent problems in the Campbell household.

"I haven't seen your friend Lizzie all summer," she commented, thinking of the chubby, giggly blonde who had been Brandy's shadow for months. "Is she out of town?"

Brandy shrugged again. "Nah. She's kind of pi—er, mad at me."

"I'm sorry to hear that."

"She's all, like, jealous or something because I've been too busy to spend much time with her lately. Jeez, I don't know how she thinks I got enough hours to work almost every evening and spend time with Marlin and hang out with her, too. I told her maybe we could go shop or something when Marlin plays basketball at the Y on Monday nights, but she's all, like, that's not enough. Just as well, I guess. Marlin don't really like her, anyway. He says she's too all about herself—and obviously he's right."

Although Cecilia knew how intense teenage romances could be, it still concerned her that Brandy seemed to be obsessed with Marlin to the point of dropping her friends. She would hate to see the girl make the same mistake she had—rushing into an ill-fated teenage marriage, ending up a disillusioned young divorcée.

"You know, boyfriends come and go while you're young, but your friendships can last a lifetime," she said, almost cringing at the triteness of the remark. "Maybe you should…"

"Now you sound like Grandma," Brandy cut in irritably. "She's always trying to tell me I spend too much time with Marlin. Well, I don't care. Me and Marlin are going to get married as soon as I graduate. There won't be any more boyfriends for me."

"Oh, Brandy, I'm sure you think that now, but you're still too young to know what will happen in the next two or three years. Don't try to grow up too fast."

"I'm old enough to know what I want," Brandy insisted, sounding as though this was a familiar, and increasingly frustrating, argument for her. "No offense, Cecilia, but I don't want to end up like you, living alone and working all the time. It's okay for you, but I want a man and a family of my own. And I'm not going to let anyone come between me and Marlin, because he's the only one who really understands me."

Flinching at the words that cut much too close to her own vulnerabilities, Cecilia tried to concentrate on the danger signs hidden in Brandy's words. Something was worrying her about Brandy, and even though the girl was openly defiant of anyone who tried to give her advice, Cecilia couldn't help feeling as if she needed to say more.

But before she could think of the words, Brandy looked beyond her. "Looks like *your* boyfriend's back," she murmured.

It took Cecilia a moment to figure out what the girl had just said. And then, with her heart in her throat, she looked quickly around to find Geoff Bingham standing on the stone pathway that led around the side of the house, gazing at her over the chain-link fence.

Chapter Five

"Hi," Geoff said, his eyes locked with Cecilia's, his expression hard for her to interpret.

Hoping he hadn't overheard Brandy's comments, Cecilia set her lemonade glass on the table. "Um…hi, yourself."

"I thought I heard voices back here. Is this a bad time?"

"No. I was just having a visit with my neighbor. Brandy Campbell, this is my, er, friend, Geoff Bingham."

"Nice to meet you, Brandy."

Brandy jumped to her feet, automatically hitching at the low-riding denim shorts that hung precariously on her bony hips. "I gotta go, anyway. Marlin will be here pretty soon. We're going to the arcade so I can watch him play video games."

Which didn't sound particularly entertaining to Cecilia, but she was too busy wondering why Geoff had come back to spend much time contemplating Brandy's choice of entertainment. "Um, yeah. See you later."

"'Kay." Brandy checked Geoff out quite thoroughly as she sauntered past him. "'Bye."

"'Bye, yourself." He watched her head for the house next door, then turned back to Cecilia. "I hope I didn't interrupt anything important."

All too aware of her yard-work dishevelment, Cecilia resisted an urge to reach up and smooth her unraveling braid. "No. I was just taking a break from weeding. Would you like some lemonade?"

"Yeah. Sure."

Standing and picking up her tray, she nodded toward the back door. "Let's go inside."

Whatever he had come to say, she thought it best not to discuss it out here, where there was the possibility of being overheard. He moved to open the door for her, and it was impossible for her to walk past him without her shoulder brushing him. Even that brief, rather impersonal contact made her pulse rate increase.

So much for convincing herself that she had already put last night behind her.

Setting the tray on the counter, she heard Geoff close the back door. She wasn't able to look at him just yet, so she busied herself by opening a cabinet and reaching for a glass.

Geoff rested a hand on her arm. "Cecilia?"

"Yes?"

"I don't really want any lemonade."

"You don't like lemonade, either?" she asked, referring to his comment about the coffee the night before.

"I like lemonade. I just don't want any right now."

She closed the cabinet and turned to face him, his hand still resting on her arm. "I didn't expect you to come back today."

"I didn't expect to be back," he admitted.

"So why…?"

"I wanted to talk to you."

She felt her cheeks warm. "If you've come to discuss the proposition I made to you earlier, it isn't necessary. I told you to forget about it."

"Have *you* forgotten about it?"

"If you mean, have I realized that I made a mistake discussing it with you, the answer is yes. It was an impulse that I should have stopped to think about before blurting it out to you. If I had, I would have realized what a crazy idea it was."

"So you aren't going to try to…well, to conceive, after all?"

She lifted her chin. "I didn't say that. If I'm ever going to have a child, I'll have to do something about it very soon."

"With someone else."

Her cheeks burned hotter. "Despite my indiscretion this morning, my reproductive choices are personal. I would rather not discuss them with you any further."

He eyed her moodily. "Do you have someone else in mind?"

"Geoff!"

"Well, do you?"

Jerking her arm away from his grasp, she whirled

to pace. "No. But I'm not giving up on my dream. If it means mortgaging my house for treatments or hanging out at singles bars or whatever I have to do, I will have a child. I can't accept that I won't ever be a mother."

She wasn't sure what, exactly, she had said to bring a scowl to his face and an edge to his voice. "It sounds as if you've made up your mind."

"I have."

He nodded. "Then so have I."

She studied him in confusion. "What do you mean?"

"I've decided to help you."

There was something decidedly surreal about calmly discussing the making of a child as if it were just another business transaction, Cecilia thought a very short while later. She and Geoff had moved to the living room to continue their conversation. As she had led him in, she had tried to hide the fact that her knees had gone suddenly weak when he had announced so abruptly and unexpectedly that he had decided to help her conceive a child. Now she wondered if he had referred to his earlier offer to help her financially with the process of artificial insemination or in vitro fertilization, rather than a more, um, active role in the conception.

"When you said you've decided to help me, what exactly did you mean?" she asked, deciding that the best way to clear up the confusion was simply to ask.

Geoff had settled onto the end of her couch closest to the chair she had chosen for herself. Clean shaven and casually dressed in a green polo shirt and pressed khakis, he looked relaxed enough sitting there facing her, but she could see the faint lines of strain around the corners of his mouth, indicating he wasn't quite as casual about all this as he seemed.

He leaned slightly toward her as he spoke. "I've done a lot of thinking about what you said this morning. You said you aren't sure you want to marry at this stage in your life—and I understand that completely. As I told you, I've been under a lot of pressure to get married, and it doesn't interest me now, either. I just don't want to make myself answerable to another adult when it already seems like I spend my whole life trying to please too many people."

"That makes perfect sense to me. I've felt that way many times."

He nodded. "So you understand that my first reaction when you made your request this morning was negative. It seemed as though you were asking me to take on the responsibility for two more people—a child and its mother."

That brought her chin up. "I thought I made it clear that I take care of myself—just as I intend to take care of my child."

Geoff held up a hand in a conciliatory gesture. "I said it seemed that way at first. The more I thought about it, the more I decided I believed you when you said you had no ulterior motives."

She wasn't sure if she was pleased that he had come to that conclusion or still rather insulted that he'd ever doubted her. "You decided correctly."

"I'm prepared to help you get what you want, but not quite the way you outlined it this morning. I have a couple of conditions of my own."

She frowned warily. "I told you this morning that I'm prepared to sign anything you want. Have your attorneys draw something up, if you like. I don't want a penny of your—"

He shook his head and held up a hand again, looking impatient this time. "Just listen, okay?"

Clenching her hands in her lap, she nodded.

Geoff rested his forearms on his thighs as he leaned even closer to her, his expression grave. "Women aren't the only ones with biological clocks, you know. I wouldn't mind having a kid, either, preferably while I'm still young enough to throw a ball or go for a hike or teach my child to swim and ride a bike. And since I'm in no hurry to marry—and I don't see that changing in the foreseeable future—your idea sounds like a solution for both of us."

She could feel the tension mounting inside her as she considered the ramifications of his words.

"I don't want to make a child and then walk away from it, in fact, there's no way I'm going to do that. But what I would consider is a joint custody arrangement. We have a child, and we raise it together...sort of."

"That isn't—" she cleared her throat "—that isn't at all what I had in mind."

"I know. You were hoping to raise this child completely on your own. I think I've made it clear I'm not interested in that sort of arrangement. But think about it, Cecilia. I'm offering the best of both worlds. A father for your child—an active father, not just a sperm donor. Financial assistance. Someone to turn to when you need to talk about a problem."

"But I—"

"I wouldn't interfere with your personal life," he assured her quickly. "And I'm still going to be on the road a lot—that's the nature of my job—so you'll still have the bulk of the day-to-day responsibilities of child rearing. But I can promise that any time you need me—any time my child needs me—I'll move heaven and earth to be there."

Her fingers knotted, causing her knuckles to ache with the strain. "I don't know, Geoff. What you're suggesting means you and I would be involved, at least in some ways, for a long time."

"Eighteen years, at a minimum," he agreed evenly, and she noticed that his left hand went to the back of his neck in the gesture she already recognized signaled his tension. This wasn't easy for him, either, she realized. "When you think about it, it's not really much different from divorced parents who come to an amicable agreement about joint custody. It's actually better for us, because we'd skip the ugly fighting and breaking-up phases and go straight to the point where we work out a plan that's best for our child."

Our child. The words seemed to echo in the room, and for the first time it felt as though they were discussing more than a hypothetical possibility. This was real, she thought dazedly—or it could be. He was offering her exactly what she wanted, though certainly with a few complications she hadn't expected. And now she wondered if she had let impulse lead her into making a huge mistake.

"Well?" Geoff prompted, studying her face as if trying to read her thoughts.

She gazed back at him and suddenly found herself

picturing a little boy with Geoff's clear hazel eyes and thick, brown hair. A little boy who would probably love to have a dad—just as Eric would have given anything as a boy to have a father in his life, she realized abruptly.

Maybe she had been selfish in wanting to deny her baby a father. And yet she doubted that Geoff would be as actively involved as he rashly predicted in the excitement of the moment. Once the novelty of the idea wore off and the reality of diapers and colic and tantrums and daily worries set in, Geoff would probably disappear—as had the men in her past. As he'd said himself, he traveled a lot, anyway, so she wouldn't have to worry about him being too visible in her life. And she would have the baby she had dreamed of for so long.

She couldn't deny that Geoff's genes were certainly arranged in a spectacular pattern, she thought, eyeing him with a silent sigh.

"This is the only deal I can offer," Geoff said when she continued to stare at him. "We compromise—or we forget the whole thing."

Finding her voice, she asked quietly, "You really think I would be a good mother? The kind of mother you would want to raise your child?"

For the first time since he'd appeared on her pathway, he smiled. "I have no doubt that you will be a wonderful mother. You helped raised Eric, didn't you? He certainly turned out okay."

Geoff seemed to know every one of her weaknesses. A compliment about her little brother was guaranteed to work with her every time.

Maybe she should be worried that he seemed to

know her so well after so short a time. But the truth was she felt strangely the same way about him. For some reason they understood each other. Had from the beginning. Their friendship was new, but it had gotten off to a wonderful start. And suddenly it didn't seem like such a bad idea to be friends with her child's father.

"I, um, suppose you want to think about this a bit longer. Before we actually commit to anything, I mean," she said.

"I'll be in town for about another month, and then I'll have to take off on business again. I'm not sure when I'll be back. So unless you want to wait until my next trip home—"

"I'm tired of waiting," Cecilia said with feeling. "It feels like I've been waiting forever."

Geoff stood and walked slowly toward her chair. "You realize, of course, that it sometimes takes a while to get results with this sort of thing."

She rose to gaze up at him. "Yes, I'm aware of that."

"I tend to be an overachiever when I'm working toward a goal. Single-minded, almost."

"I've been accused of being the same," she admitted, tilting her head back as he moved even closer, so that he towered over her.

He lifted a hand to her cheek, his thumb tracing the line of her jaw. "Just so you'll know, I'm willing to give this my best effort. As often as possible—as many times as it takes."

Her smile felt a bit shaky. Uncharacteristically shy. "That's very noble of you."

His other hand rose so that he was cupping her face

between his palms. He leaned so close to her that she could feel his breath ruffling her hair when he murmured, ''I just wanted to reassure you that you've picked the right guy for the job.''

Before she could tell him that she had already reached that conclusion for herself, his mouth was on hers.

The heavy wooden door to Geoff's condominium loomed in front of Cecilia later that evening. Because of the impressive security in the building, he knew she had arrived, but she hesitated before ringing the bell. It felt like her last chance to change her mind and make a dash for sanity, but when it came right down to it, she just didn't want to go.

She had been perfectly willing for Geoff to simply stay at her place earlier. She would have prepared a meal for them—spaghetti, maybe, or a quick casserole—followed by...well, by the first step in their get-Cecilia-pregnant campaign. But Geoff had vetoed that plan, insisting, to her surprise, that he would cook for her, instead. At his place.

He had explained that he wanted this night to be special. Cecilia had wondered then, as she wondered now, if he had really been giving her time to rethink her decision. To change her mind, if she wanted. By having her come to his place, he was giving her the option to leave whenever she wanted.

She smoothed her hands down the sides of the mid-calf-length black knit skirt she had paired with a sleeveless top in a purple-and-black geometric print. Her freshly washed hair was pinned up into a neat roll, and she had applied her makeup very carefully.

Quite a contrast to her disheveled and rather grubby appearance earlier, she decided in satisfaction.

He'd caught her off guard earlier, but this time she was prepared. No more stammering or blushing. Her intention now was to act like the mature, competent, confident woman her carefully groomed exterior proclaimed her to be. She was a woman with a plan, and she would not allow last-minute qualms to get in her way.

Squaring her shoulders and holding her chin high, she reached out to ring his bell with a proudly steady hand.

Geoff opened the door. One look at him standing there in a crisp white shirt and beautifully tailored dark slacks made her mouth go dry. And now her hands were trembling. So much for calm and composure, she thought with a silent sigh of exasperation.

He gave her a smile that made her heart race even faster. "You look beautiful."

With an inward struggle for composure, she said, "Thank you."

Stepping back, he motioned her inside. "Come in. Dinner's almost ready."

She looked around with discreet curiosity as she entered his home. She had never visited one of these exclusive condominiums before. From the spectacular mountain view to the obviously professionally decorated interior, the condo spoke of money and social status. It was a very different setting from her modest little middle-class house, but she still preferred her own home.

There was something rather cold and impersonal about Geoff's condo. It felt like...well, like a hotel room, she decided, glancing at a vase full of neatly arranged, hothouse flowers.

Because etiquette demanded it, she said, "This is very nice."

"Thanks. But to be honest, I've had very little to do with it. I'm not here enough to put much of myself into the place."

Glancing again around the cream-on-cream room with its elegant touches of gleaming woods, polished brass and green-veined marble, she asked curiously, "What would you change if you could put yourself into it?"

Geoff raised his eyebrows as if he'd never actually asked himself that question before. "I, um, well, I guess it would look a bit more like your place."

She was tempted to roll her eyes. "You would fill your fancy condo with secondhand furniture and handmade decorations?"

"I would try to make it look like a home," he corrected her, "and not just a designer's showcase."

She smiled at him. "I'm pretty sure that was a compliment."

"It was meant to be."

A timer buzzed in another room. Geoff turned in that direction. "I'd better take care of that."

"Can I help?"

"You can keep me company while I finish up."

She followed him into a black granite and stainless steel kitchen that looked as though it belonged in a magazine dedicated to gourmet cuisine. This room, at least, showed signs of use. Pots simmered on the six-burner stove, utensils were scattered on the counters, and something had been spilled on the stone floor.

Geoff spotted the spill at the same time she did. He grabbed a paper towel and bent to wipe it up. "I tend to be sort of messy when I cook," he said as he straightened.

"Whatever you've prepared, it smells heavenly."

He opened the oven door. "Rosemary chicken, rice with almonds and peas, orange-glazed carrots and crusty wheat rolls. I bought the rolls, by the way. They're the heat-and-serve kind."

"Everything sounds delicious. Are you sure there's nothing I can do?"

"You can grab that basket of rolls and follow me."

He led her into a small but elegant dining room, and once again she was struck by how much trouble he had gone to for her this evening. Candles burned on the table and on an antique sideboard she'd have given her eyeteeth for. Mounds of fresh flowers had been arranged in crystal bowls. The table was perfectly set with snowy linens, white china and gleaming silver.

A housekeeper? she wondered. Or had he done all of this himself?

Geoff moved to hold her chair for her, and she was romantic enough to be touched by his efforts. It was a scene set for seduction, made even more special because it hadn't been necessary. The outcome of this evening was pretty much a sure thing—and would have been even if their meal had consisted of burgers from a fast-food drive-through.

Geoff seemed completely comfortable during their meal. The perfect host, charming, witty and relaxed. Oddly enough, Cecilia grew more nervous as the evening progressed. Because he had gone to the trouble of providing brandied fruits for dessert, she accepted a dish, but she could eat only a few bites.

"Is something wrong, Cecilia?"

She looked up from her barely touched fruit to give Geoff a smile that she hoped looked more natural than it felt. "Not at all. I'm just getting full. Dinner was excellent, by the way. You're a very good cook."

"Thank you. My repertoire is a bit limited, but my mother made sure I knew my way around a kitchen. Even though we had cooks and housekeepers while I was growing up, Mom said everyone should be able to prepare a meal, sew on a button and run a vacuum cleaner."

"Your mother was a very practical woman."

"Yes, she was. It was important to her that Mari and I would not grow up spoiled, even if we were fortunate enough to have a privileged upbringing. She was determined that we would understand exactly how lucky we were, so we spent every Christmas helping her with her charity projects. Working in soup kitchens, delivering food baskets and toys to homes that were little more than drafty shacks, visiting nursing homes and hospital wards."

"We had a tradition in our family, too," Cecilia mused. "We each contributed money from our allowances and paychecks to donate to the homeless shelter each Christmas. We usually had a rather modest holiday, ourselves, but Mother wanted us to understand that there were always people who had less."

"Your mother must have worked very hard to support you and your brother."

"Too hard," Cecilia admitted with a sigh. "It seemed as if she was always working. After my father died so young and Eric's worthless father took off before Eric was even born, Mother decided she couldn't depend on anyone ever again. Except me, of course. By the time I was twelve, I was responsible for Eric's care. I fed him, bathed him, dressed him, read him his bedtime stories, tucked him into bed. I'm sure that's why I still tend to be overly maternal with him, giving him entirely too much advice and too many unsolicited opinions.''

''I have a feeling he is more appreciative of your concern for him than resentful.''

''Most of the time, yes. He lets me know when I cross the line into meddling—not that I always take the hint,'' she added with a faint smile.

''Who took care of him while you were in school?''

''A series of baby-sitters and day-care providers. The best care Mother could arrange for him.''

''I want to assure you that you'll never have to work that hard to support our child. I'll make sure of that.''

Cecilia set her dessert fork down abruptly, making no further pretense at eating. ''I told you, I'm not after your money. That has absolutely nothing to do with my reasons for asking you to help me.''

He already had a hand up to appease her. ''I wasn't implying anything about your motives. I simply wanted to remind you again that I'm not anything like Eric's father. I won't leave you to shoulder the financial burdens alone, and my child won't have to grow up with the knowledge that his father had no interest in him.''

Cecilia shifted restlessly in her chair. ''I suppose I

have been a bit selfish in that respect. I know the ideal situation is to provide two caring parents for a child. But I've already explained that the clinic day-care center will let me be more visible and active than my mother was able to be with Eric. And the child will have Eric and Hannah and their baby for extended family. An uncle, an aunt and a playmate."

"Now he—or she—will also have a devoted father. Another aunt. A grandfather and a great-grandmother. Family he'll share with Eric's child, of course, since Hannah is my cousin. It's a bit convoluted, but I believe we can make this work. I know it isn't what you had in mind originally, but surely you can see it's better for everyone involved, especially the child."

"Once I get past my knee-jerk reluctance to share my baby with anyone, I do see the advantages," she admitted.

His smile could almost be described as sweet—if such a flowery adjective could be applied to a man so undeniably virile and masculine. "I won't ever try to take your child away from you, Cecilia. We're partners in this adventure, not competitors. And *I'll* sign anything you like to set your mind at ease about that."

She gave a self-conscious little laugh. "Stop reading my mind. I suppose it does concern me a bit that our social and financial circumstances are so different. It gives you advantages that I can't help but be nervous about."

"I won't abuse your trust in me," he vowed again. "I'm sure we'll have some disagreements about child rearing—we're both the independent and assertive types, or we wouldn't be so successful in our respective careers—but we'll work everything out to our mutual satisfaction. I can negotiate and make compromises when I'm working toward something important."

"So can I."

He held out a hand to her. "Then we're agreed. Our baby is going to have two parents who will always put his—or her—interests ahead of their own."

She laid her hand in his. "So you think we're doing the right thing?"

His fingers closing warmly around hers, he smiled a bit crookedly this time. "Beats the hell out of me. I just know it feels right now."

"You could sound a little more confident."

He chuckled. "I don't have a crystal ball, Cecilia. We don't even know that we can have a child together. All I know is that I'll be the best father I can be and that you'll make a great mother. If you're still certain this is what you want—"

"It is," she cut in quickly. "It's all I've wanted for a very long time."

"Then let's go for it."

She inhaled deeply, then released the breath in a long sigh. The decision had been made. There was no going back now. She could hardly believe that she was finally taking steps to make sure her most cherished lifelong dream could come true.

Chapter Six

Cecilia might have worried that nerves would inter-fere with their lovemaking this time. After all, it was different when there was a goal other than simple pleasure at stake. If Geoff had been at all tense or awkward, she would have understood and forgiven him.

Instead, he seduced her as if it were the first time again. As if nothing mattered more to him than her pleasure. As if there were nowhere in the world he would rather be, nothing he would rather be doing than making love with her on this summer night.

His kisses went from gentle to passionate, his movements from practiced to impetuous. He was an amazing lover—generous, thorough, patient. Even when he was obviously driven by an overwhelming need for climax, he made sure she found her own release before he gave in to his.

Lying sated and exhausted beside him afterward, she wondered at his control. Was everything he did always so calculated? Even his seemingly impulsive decision to help her conceive had come after a day of thought and consideration, during which she would bet he had deliberated every angle and potential repercussion. This was very likely the most rebellious and nonconformist action he had ever taken, and even in that he had made it clear that he intended to be fully responsible for and committed to the child they were making.

"Geoff?"

The arm behind her tightened a bit as he drew her more snugly against him. "Mmm?"

He sounded half-asleep. As lazy and satisfied as she was. She couldn't help smiling a little before asking, "What will your family think about this?"

He lifted his head from the pillow, casting a glance downward at their nude, intimately entwined bodies. "About *this?*"

She giggled. "I meant about you having a child with me. If you intend to claim the child as your own—"

"Which I do."

She nodded. "So what will they think about you having a baby with Eric's sister? One of their employees. A woman who, by the way, is considerably older than you."

"You keep mentioning your age. Does it really bother you that you're thirty-seven and I'm thirty-two? It's not that great a difference, you know. And they are, after all, only numbers."

"I know. But I can't help but think your family won't approve."

"I won't lie to you, Cecilia, they're going to think I've lost my mind. At first. As I've told you, they want me to get married. Start a family in the traditional way. They don't understand why I won't let them fix me up with a nice girl with the right connections. They'll understand my wanting a child—after all, I've been raised to appreciate the value of family—but they won't believe I'm going about it the right way."

It was what she had expected, of course, but still…

"Don't worry about it," he said, then brushed a kiss across her forehead. "They'll come around. If there's one thing my grandmother loves, it's babies. And Dad will be tickled to be a grandfather, even if it isn't exactly the way he had envisioned. To be honest, he has begun to wonder aloud if he's ever going to have grandkids."

"Still—"

"Cecilia. It's my life. My choice. For once my family will just have to accept that. And they will."

Once again she thought she heard the faintest trace of rebellion in his voice, as if this was the first time in a very long while that he had risked openly defying his family. As if he rather enjoyed the prospect.

"And if you do find that nice girl with the 'right' connections that you want to marry?" she couldn't help asking, keeping her voice carefully neutral. "What do you expect her to think about you having a child?"

"I have no interest in getting married, can't think of anyone I would want to marry, but if it should ever happen that I meet someone I feel that way about, she'll just have to accept the decisions I made before I met her. The same holds true for you, you know. You may well meet someone, yourself...."

She was shaking her head before he even finished speaking. "Not likely. I'm too...well, I won't say old, but too set in my ways to be interested in marriage now. I like making my own decisions. Handling my own problems. Setting my own priorities."

"Some of that will change when you have a child."

"True. But I'll still be in charge of my own household."

"Your marriage must have been a very unhappy one."

She hadn't realized she had revealed quite so much. "Yes, it was. But I'm not bitter or angry. Just realistic."

He shifted to lean over her, his expression both grave and tender at the same time. "Any man who would make you unhappy—who was not respectful of your needs and your dreams, who tried to break your valiant and independent spirit, who didn't value you for the strong, capable woman you are—was not worth the time you wasted with him."

She grinned and slid her arms around his neck. "You know what? You are absolutely right."

A gleam of satisfaction and renewed desire warmed his beautiful eyes. "I usually am," he murmured as he lowered his head to hers.

Cecilia refused to spend the night. It was quite late when Geoff escorted her to his door. "Are you sure you won't let me follow you home?"

"I'll be fine," she assured him. "I've got the kind of job that often takes me out in the middle of the night, remember?"

"You could call me when you get there—just so I'll know you're safe."

She wrinkled her nose. "Don't start practicing your fathering skills on me, Geoff. I'm quite capable of taking care of myself."

He laughed and looped an arm around her shoulders for a quick hug. "I've never met anyone quite as stubbornly independent as you—with the possible exception of my sister. So will we see each other tomorrow?"

"I have plans for lunch, but I'm free tomorrow evening. Unless you have other plans?"

He shook his head. "How about taking in a movie? I haven't seen any of the big summer blockbusters this year. It's been forever since I've been to a theater for some popcorn and a couple of hours of mindless entertainment."

She chuckled. "Actually, I did sort of want to see that new superhero film. Eric loved it, but his taste in film is sometimes questionable, so it could be awful."

"Let's go find out, shall we? I have to admit, I was hoping to see that one, too. Have I mentioned I had a serious comic book addiction as a kid?"

"No, you didn't."

"My mother finally sent me to a twelve-step program to break me of the habit. She called it school. I learned to appreciate other types of literature, but I kept a stash of comics hidden under my mattress."

"No girlie magazines?"

"I eventually worked my way up to those," he confessed, looking not the least embarrassed. "I outgrew them both about the time I was able to grow a mustache. But I still have a soft spot for the comics. So I'd like to see the movie, even though it will probably make a mess of the original story, as those films so often do."

"Then, it's a date." And then, because that sounded too cozy for the relationship they had agreed upon, she said quickly, "Well, not a date, exactly, but a plan. I mean…"

"It's a date," Geoff interrupted firmly and pressed a kiss on her still-parted lips before opening his door. "Drive carefully, Cecilia. I'll call you tomorrow to arrange a time."

She drove home in a haze of bemusement that her life had changed so drastically in the past twenty-four hours. And her state of mind was so mixed up that she wasn't sure which was harder to believe—that she had a date with Geoff Bingham or that she could even now be carrying his child.

"Are you sure there's nothing I can fix for you while I'm here, CeCe? Didn't you say you've got a squeaky hinge in the bathroom that's been driving you nuts?"

Cecilia smiled lovingly across the dining table at her brother, who, along with his fiancée, had joined her for Sunday lunch. Eric had called her CeCe from the time he had learned to speak, and it was certainly too late to try to change that habit now. She wouldn't be at all surprised if his child called her "Aunt

CeCe.'' Oh, well, she supposed she could live with that as long as Eric looked this happy, she mused, watching the adoring look he gave Hannah.

"I took care of the squeaky hinge myself. A little shot of oil was all it needed."

Eric frowned. "What about the step that was coming loose on the back porch?"

"I found a hammer and a nail, and I fixed it myself. I have paid attention to a few of your maintenance lessons, you know."

Hannah laughed. "Looks as if you aren't quite as indispensable as you think, Eric. Your sister is perfectly capable of looking after herself."

"She always has been," Eric admitted. "I just like to delude myself occasionally into thinking that she needs me."

"I will always need you," Cecilia assured him. "Just not necessarily as an on-call handyman. You have your own life now, and it's about to get very busy," she added with a meaningful glance at Hannah's rapidly expanding tummy.

Resting a hand on the bulge, Hannah sighed a little. "None too soon, as far as I'm concerned."

Cecilia smiled. "Between the wedding and childbirth classes and setting up your household, the next eight weeks are going to pass more quickly than you can imagine. It won't be long at all before you're holding that baby in your arms."

And maybe, if she was lucky, she would hold a baby of her own before this time next year, she thought wistfully.

"So, CeCe, Hannah and I were thinking about going to the park this evening to hear the bluegrass band that's scheduled to perform. Would you like to join us?''

''Thank you, but I have other plans,'' she said, busying herself by scooping another spoonful of peas onto his plate. ''Here, have some more of these. You never eat enough vegetables. You'll have to keep an eye on that, Hannah. I swear he would live on junk food and candy if we let him.''

Eric cleared his throat. ''I am an adult.''

''So eat like one.''

Hannah laughed again.

''What plans do you have this evening?'' Eric asked, turning the conversation back to Cecilia.

She should have known her ploy to change the subject wouldn't have worked. Eric was like a dog with a juicy bone when his curiosity was aroused. ''I'm going to a movie.''

''Alone?''

''Eric,'' Hannah murmured, ''your sister would tell you her plans if she wanted you to know them.''

''Hey, if she can monitor my diet, I can ask a few questions about her life,'' he retorted. ''Who're you going to the movie with, CeCe?''

She sighed. Might as well answer him, she told herself in resignation. The way gossip spread through this town, he would hear it eventually, anyway. ''Geoff Bingham.''

Hannah's eyes widened. Eric looked startled. ''Geoff Bingham? You mean it was true that you two had dinner together after the reception Friday evening? I thought that was just a case of mistaken identity.''

"How could you possibly have heard about that already?"

"Oh, you know. Someone saw you and told someone else who told— But that isn't important. I didn't even believe it."

"Well, it's true," Cecilia admitted. "Geoff was hungry at the reception, and so was I, so we had dinner together at Melinda's."

"And tonight you're seeing a movie together."

"Yes. Neither of us had plans for the evening, so…"

No way was she telling her brother what she and Geoff were really up to. There would be time enough for that when—*if,* she corrected herself cautiously— it became a fait accompli. After it was too late for Eric to try to change her mind, which she had no doubt that he would do.

"What's going on?" Eric asked bluntly. "You're dating a Bingham? Aren't you the one who warned me about getting involved with one of them?"

"For heaven's sake, Eric." Feeling her cheeks warm, Cecilia cast a quick, apologetic look at Hannah, who looked more embarrassed than offended. "You know I'm delighted that you're marrying Hannah."

"Of course. Once you got to know her you saw how wonderful she is. And, of course, she wasn't really raised a Bingham, since she was a teenager when she found out that Billy Bingham was her father. But Geoff—he's a Bingham to his neatly polished wingtips. I wouldn't have thought he was your type at all."

"I'm not marrying him, Eric, I'm simply taking in

a movie with him,'' she replied. Among other things, she silently added.

Eric didn't look particularly reassured. ''But—''

''Goodness, the baby certainly is active this afternoon,'' Hannah said suddenly, pressing her hand to her tummy again. ''Feels as if there's a jazzercise class taking place in there.''

To Cecilia's great relief, and obviously exactly as Hannah had intended, that drew Eric's attention away from his sister's social life. He had to reach over to feel the baby's movements, which led to more talk about prenatal care and delivery preparations, which led again to the plans for the simple wedding that would take place very soon.

Cecilia knew her brother had allowed himself to be distracted. He hadn't forgotten her impending date with Geoff. He confirmed that suspicion as he and Hannah prepared to walk out the front door a little while later.

''Watch yourself with Bingham this evening, you hear?'' he warned his sister after kissing her cheek. ''The guy practically oozes charm. He's the family politician and has a way of getting anything he wants.''

''Don't worry. I know exactly what Geoff is like,'' Cecilia replied lightly. And since Geoff's wants at the moment were closely aligned with her own, she hoped sincerely that Eric was right about Geoff always getting his way.

Still looking a bit fretful, Eric allowed Hannah to tow him away, leaving Cecilia to get ready for another interesting evening with Geoff.

*　*　*

Geoff found himself approaching Cecilia's front door with a spring in his step that made him feel strangely like an eager teenager. After a rather tense day, an evening in Cecilia's warm, pleasant and un-demanding company sounded awfully nice.

And speaking of teenagers…

He raised a hand in greeting to the redhead who had just hurried out of the house next door in response to an imperative horn blast from a long-haired boy in a battered brown pickup truck spotted with patches of gray primer. The girl quickly returned Geoff's wave, then jumped into the truck, which was peeling away from the curb almost before she could close her door.

So much for the social niceties of modern teenage dating, Geoff thought with a glance at the small bou-quet of flowers in his hand.

Cecilia seemed delighted by the offering. "These weren't necessary, but thank you," she said, burying her face in the fragrant blooms for a moment.

Grinning, Geoff motioned toward the house next door. "Guess I could have just pulled up to the curb and blown the horn. Seemed to work for your neigh-bor."

Cecilia sighed and shook her head. "Marlin refuses to get out of his truck when he picks Brandy up for their dates. She says it's because her grandparents don't like him, but that behavior certainly doesn't en-dear him to them."

"Is he the one who gave her the shiner?"

Cecilia seemed startled by the question. "Her bruised cheek, you mean? She told me she did that while playing a game of catch. She didn't get her glove up fast enough.''

"Mmm." It hadn't looked like a softball injury to Geoff, but he supposed Cecilia knew what was going on next door better than he did. "Ready for the movie?"

"Just let me put these in water," she said, turning quickly with the flowers. "You can wait in the living room. I'll be right back."

Closing the front door behind him, he caught her arm to detain her for a moment. Before she could ask what he was doing, he planted a long, firm kiss on her lips.

"That was just to hold me over until later," he murmured when he released her.

Her expression held just a hint of reproach. "You are a fresh one, Mr. Bingham."

"Want me to stop?"

With a smile brilliant enough to make him blink, she murmured, "Don't you dare."

He was grinning when she turned to walk away, adding a seductive swish of her hips to her movements. He really liked this woman.

There were only two movie theaters in the immediate area—downtown Binghamton's old-style movie house, the Bijou, which offered a selection of new and classic family films, and a more modern four-screen metroplex in an adjoining town. Geoff took Cecilia to the latter, since that was where the super-hero film was playing.

There was a good-size crowd at the theater on this nice summer evening, and once again there were a

few who obviously recognized both Cecilia and
Geoff. Once again they exchanged nods of greeting
without getting entangled in conversation. Cecilia
couldn't imagine what the gossips were making of her
second public appearance with Geoff, but she
wouldn't worry about that for now.

They shared a buttered popcorn during the movie,
their hands brushing with almost suspicious frequency
as they reached for popcorn at the same time. Funny
how Geoff always seemed to be hungry at the same
time she was, she thought with a glance at his blandly
innocent profile.

When the popcorn was gone, he abandoned sub-
terfuge and simply took her hand in his, entwining
their fingers in a loose, warm clasp. He sat closely
enough that their knees brushed, and even through the
fabric of his jeans and her chinos, she felt the impact
of the contact.

It was a good thing the action-packed and plot-thin
film required little thought or attention, Cecilia decided. Geoff had her so addled that she couldn't even
remember the names of the characters.

Even though they had both agreed their relationship
was temporary and based on a specific purpose that
had little to do with romance, he still seemed to enjoy
these nice gestures. Flowers, dates, holding hands. A
charming man, this Geoff Bingham—the family politician, she reminded herself.

Still, she couldn't help but enjoy his attentions.
What woman wouldn't?

As the film came to an end—finally—Geoff lifted
their hands to his lips, brushing a kiss across her

knuckles. "My place or yours?" he murmured into her ear.

"Mine's a bit closer," she whispered back, as anxious as he seemed to be to be out of the public eye.

The credits rolled and the theater lights came up, and Geoff pulled Cecilia to her feet. "Let's see how fast we can get there."

It sounded like a good plan to her.

Chapter Seven

Because of the usual rush for the exits, it took Cecilia and Geoff a few minutes to get into the aisle. They had almost reached the back of the rapidly emptying theater when Cecilia noticed a very pregnant young woman still seated about halfway down one of the rows of high-backed seats. The woman was doubled over, apparently in pain, while an anxious-looking young man sat beside her, talking to her.

Cecilia had to stop. Stepping around one of the theater employees who had entered to pick up trash between screenings, she walked sideways down the aisle to get closer to the woman while Geoff waited curiously behind her.

"Is everything okay?" she asked the woman, who was moaning quietly in a way that had Cecilia's midwifery instincts kicking into overtime.

The young man, whom she would guess to be about twenty-two, looked around quickly. "Katie— my girlfriend—isn't feeling good. Maybe she shouldn't have eaten so much candy during the movie."

Cecilia bent down to check the pregnant woman— girl, she corrected herself when the extremely pale Katie looked up at her. This mother-to-be couldn't be older than seventeen. "Where does it hurt?"

Katie's brown eyes swam in tears. "Everywhere."

"When is your due date?"

"Next month. The fifteenth."

Three weeks away, Cecilia figured rapidly. "My name is Cecilia Mendoza, and I'm a nurse-midwife. Tell me about the pain. Is it steady or does it come in waves?"

Looking relieved to have an expert at hand, Katie whispered, "It hurts all the time, but it comes in waves, too. They start in my back and move around to the front. I...I don't think it was the candy."

"I don't think so, either," Cecilia murmured, watching as Katie stiffened against another sharp pain. "How long has this been going on?"

"About...about an hour. Maybe a little more, wasn't it, Rusty?"

"I told her we could leave if she didn't feel good, but she wanted to see the end of the movie," Rusty said defensively. "She said it might be a long time before we'd get a chance to come to another movie because of the baby and all."

Geoff leaned closer to Cecilia. "Should I call an ambulance?"

Because Katie had already doubled into another contraction, Cecilia nodded. "Tell them to hurry."

Geoff already had his cell phone to his ear when Cecilia turned back to Rusty. "Let's see if we can get her to the aisle. I can't get to her now to see what's happening."

Bobbing his sandy head in assent, Rusty got on one side of Katie, grabbed her arm, and yanked upward. Wincing, Cecilia placed a hand on his shoulder. "Gently."

"Oh. Yeah, sure. So you think she's like in labor or something?"

Katie let out a moan that ended as a near wail.

"I think it's a definite possibility," Cecilia replied.

"Oh, man."

Staggering to her feet, Katie took a few halting steps, then cried out again. "It really hurts, Miss Mendoza."

They were attracting attention now, as the theater employees stopped their tasks to gawk at them. Geoff moved forward. "Here, let me help."

Without further hesitation, he bent to sweep Katie into his arms. "Where do you want her?" he asked, not even appearing to strain beneath the weight of the heavily pregnant young woman.

At least this theater was pretty much empty for the moment, she thought—and could stay that way until after the emergency crew had arrived, she decided abruptly. "Let's just lay her in the aisle. Randy, sit cross-legged so we can rest her head in your lap. Geoff, let the manager know what's going on so they can clear a path for the emergency crew. Were you given an estimated time of arrival?"

"There was a multicar wreck on the mountain highway on the other side of the county," he replied as he helped arrange Katie as comfortably as possible. "The dispatcher said there could be a delay. Want me to get my car? We could probably get her to the clinic faster than the ambulance."

Cecilia bit back a grumble. Poverty-stricken Merlyn County was a victim of difficult financial times, and emergency services had suffered in the resulting cutbacks. Having a state-of-the-art medical facility was a blessing, but they had to get the patients there first, she thought with familiar frustration.

She watched as Katie bowed upward, a ragged cry escaping her taut lips. "I don't think that's a good idea. I'd rather deliver a baby here, if necessary, than in the tiny back seat of your car."

"D-deliver?" Rusty stammered. "You mean the baby's coming *now?*"

"I won't know until I check." She spoke calmly, reassuringly. "Geoff, maybe you'd clear the employees out of here on your way to notify the manager? I think Katie would be more comfortable without spectators. And see if you can find some towels—paper, if necessary," she added as a dark, wet stain spread rapidly across the front of Katie's light-colored maternity jeans.

Geoff met her eyes for a moment, mutely acknowledging the seriousness of the situation, and then he efficiently took charge of the scene.

The theater manager, a stocky, auburn-haired woman in her forties with kind eyes and a brusque manner, appeared with a blanket and a couple of towels. "I heard what's happening. I keep these in my office for emergencies. I'm holding the showing of the next film until the ambulance arrives.''

"Thank you.'' Cecilia draped the blanket over Katie, who was weeping quietly now between racking, near-constant contractions. "Things seem to be moving very quickly. I'm a midwife, so I can handle things in here if you'll take care of everything out there.''

"No problem.'' The manager leaned over Katie. "You listen to this lady, honey. She'll help you till the ambulance gets here.''

Writhing and panting, Katie still managed to nod in response to the manager's maternal advice. "Yes, ma'am.''

After dashing through a curious milling crowd to the nearest bathroom, where she did the best she could to wash up with plenty of soap and warm water, Cecilia hurried back into the theater to find Katie still moaning, Rusty looking even queasier, and Geoff doing his best to keep both of them from panicking.

"You're being very brave, Katie,'' Cecilia encouraged, reaching beneath the modestly draped blanket. "I'm going to take these wet clothes off, okay? If you can lift up for me, I'll arrange these towels beneath you—the best we can do by way of a sheet for you to lie on. We'll keep the blanket draped over you so no one will see anything except me.''

Katie was arching again, her hands flailing. "I don't care. Just make it stop hurting so bad.''

"Lift your knees, sweetie. I'm going to do a quick check to see how far along you are.''

"Oh, man,'' Rusty muttered, and he had gone so

pale and glassy-eyed that Cecilia wondered how long it would be before he hit the floor in a faint.

Geoff, on the other hand, was perfectly calm. He knelt beside Katie and took her restless hands in his, looking directly into her eyes.

"Katie, do you remember that my name is Geoff?" he said, speaking loudly enough to be heard over her moans. When she nodded, he continued, "Cecilia delivers babies every day, so she knows exactly what she's doing. I want you to hold on to me and squeeze my hands if it helps when you feel pain. Rusty's going to wipe your face with the damp paper towel I just handed him, aren't you, Rusty?"

"Uh, yeah." Apparently grateful to have something useful to do, Rusty wielded the towel with more enthusiasm than finesse.

"Oh, my goodness," Cecilia said a few moments later. "This baby is in a real hurry to get here."

She suspected that Katie had been in labor longer than the hour or hour and a half she had admitted. Had the girl really been so eager to see the film, which Cecilia hadn't even considered very good? Or had she been too young and inexperienced to recognize the signs as something more than the usual discomforts of late pregnancy?

"When was your last prenatal checkup, Katie?"

Katie was too busy to answer, her face contorted as she squeezed Geoff's hands hard enough to make him wince a little. Cecilia gave him a quick smile of encouragement before looking to Rusty for an answer.

Rusty cleared his throat, his eyes darting nervously. "It's been a few months. We don't have insurance, see, and we couldn't afford to go running to the doctor all the time. Everything was fine last time she went, so we thought it would be okay to wait.''

Cecilia bit back an exasperated sigh. Money couldn't have been the only obstacle to prenatal care, since the clinic provided income-based services when lack of insurance was a factor. More likely they lacked transportation or time or simply the incentive to make the appointments. She had seen all too many deliveries complicated by lack of adequate prenatal care.

At least Katie seemed to be reasonably healthy. Her pulse was steady and strong, and she was already completely effaced and almost fully dilated, so the delivery should be relatively uncomplicated. Cecilia saw no signs of drug abuse or other health concerns— but, damn, she wished that ambulance would get here. Delivery in a theater aisle was bad enough. But doing so with absolutely no medical supplies available was even more difficult.

"Aah," Katie cried out, her entire body contracting in pain. "It hurts, Miss Mendoza. And I need to push."

Rusty blanched as pale as his white tennis shoes and began to sway. Cecilia gave Geoff a look before turning back to her duties.

"Rusty," she heard Geoff say a bit sharply. "Stay with us, you hear? Katie needs you to be strong now."

"I'll—" Rusty cleared his squeaky voice, speaking a bit more clearly next time. "I'll be strong," he promised. "I won't let you down, Katie."

"Good man," Geoff murmured, and then he smiled down at Katie again. "Just concentrate on holding that baby in your arms, okay? You've got a lot of help here.''

It didn't surprise Cecilia in the least that both Rusty and Katie seemed to find reassurance in Geoff's steady, confident manner. To be honest, she felt much the same way.

''You were absolutely amazing this evening.'' Geoff gave Cecilia a dazzling smile as he spoke, making her heart beat a little faster in reaction.

''I was simply doing my job,'' she demurred.

''No, it was more than that. You kept those kids calm, even when they were on the verge of panic. And considering the circumstances, you delivered that baby as easily as if you had all the clinic facilities at your disposal.''

Self-conscious about the praise Geoff had been heaping on her for the past hour, she tucked a strand of hair behind her ear. ''It helped that the ambulance arrived before the baby did.''

''By all of ten minutes.''

She gave a brief, tired laugh. ''True. But at least I had some professional assistance at the end.''

Snuggled beside her on her couch, Geoff kissed her forehead. ''I still thought you were amazing.''

She rested her head on his shoulder. ''You were pretty cool and collected yourself. The way you talked so reassuringly to Katie and Rusty. The way you kept her focused on you when the contractions were so strong. You sounded like a professional doula—a trained birthing coach.''

Geoff chuckled. Lifting his right hand, he flexed

the fingers a few times. "Let me tell you, that girl's got a grip. My fingers are still numb."

"You're a very handy man to have around in an emergency."

Dropping his hand to his knee, he turned his attention back to her. "So, do things like that happen to you often? How many babies have you delivered unexpectedly like that?"

"Counting this one?"

"Yes."

"One."

His eyebrows shot up in surprise. "No kidding? That was the first time?"

"Contrary to what you see on television, babies aren't often born in theaters or elevators or cabs or airplanes. I mean, sure, it happens—obviously—and I've known colleagues who made emergency deliveries before, but that was a first for me."

He pressed another kiss on her forehead. "You handled it beautifully."

"Thank you. But as I've already said, it's my job. I simply did what I'm trained to do. Even though I have to confess that I don't want to have to work under those circumstances again anytime soon. A dirty theater floor—no antiseptics or hot water or even a pair of gloves...."

She shuddered. No, she didn't want to go through that again. She was grateful that the paramedics had arrived before the baby, being on hand with medical supplies and IVs to take charge of Katie's care while Cecilia had wrapped the screaming, apparently healthy baby boy in a sterile blanket. Somehow Rusty had survived the ordeal without passing out, a feat for which Geoff had praised him generously.

Rather than being annoyed by the delay of their movie, the crowd in the lobby had broken into applause when Katie and the baby had been wheeled to the waiting ambulance. So much for making a discreet exit, Cecilia had thought as she and Geoff had made their way to his car through a barrage of questions and congratulations.

They'd only arrived at her house a short while earlier, collapsing onto the couch as soon as they'd walked in. Their simple movie date had turned into an exhausting and emotionally draining event, Cecilia mused, and they both needed a little time to recharge.

Geoff seemed to still be preoccupied with their adventure. "Do all newborn babies look like that? All gooey and wrinkled and sort of purple?"

"Pretty much."

"Oh. I thought maybe their kid was just... homely."

Amused, Cecilia tilted her head back to smile at him. "Actually, he was a rather pretty baby."

"If you say so."

"He looked like his mother, I think."

"Fortunate, considering that his father was pretty goofy looking."

She felt almost guilty for laughing. "You're terrible."

"Maybe I wasn't seeing him at his best."

"Obviously you weren't."

Settling more comfortably into the cushions, Geoff tightened his arm around Cecilia's shoulders. "That baby's got a tough road ahead of him. His parents are just kids themselves. Chances are slim they'll stay together—or that his mother will even finish high school."

"Children born to teenage mothers are much more likely to live in poverty, less likely to have health insurance, less likely to get an adequate education, and more likely to become teenage parents themselves. But...well, maybe things will work out for Rusty and Katie and their son. I hope so, anyway."

Geoff seemed to think about that for a while. And then he sighed and said, "It's been a long day."

"Did you work today?"

"Worse. I had lunch with my dad and my sister."

Raising her eyebrows, she kicked off her shoes and tucked her feet on the couch behind her. "I thought you got along well with your family."

"Oh, we get along. Everyone was just sort of grumpy today."

"Grumpy?"

"Yeah. Mari couldn't get her mind away from work. All she could talk about was the lawsuit—"

"That is worrisome," Cecilia murmured. "Poor Milla doesn't deserve that hassle."

"It's hardly good for the clinic, either. It's bad enough that all the rumors about the biomed center are threatening our endowments from local investors. Just talking about fertility research—not to mention such controversial subjects as stem-cell research— makes some people so skittish they're afraid to even be mentioned in the same context. This lawsuit couldn't have come at a worse time."

"There's always a frivolous lawsuit of some sort against a hospital, especially when obstetrics are involved. It's why so many doctors and hospitals have gotten out of the delivery business. Not that I have to explain the daunting rise in malpractice insurance to you.''

"Hardly. That's the sort of business discussion that's been taking place in my family since I was old enough to join them at the dinner table.''

"Mari's under a great deal of pressure in her job. She's allowed an occasional grumpy day.'' As for herself, Cecilia was perfectly content being a valued employee of the corporation rather than trying to fill an executive position, as her brother dreamed about doing. Her passion was delivering babies, not crunching numbers or studying spreadsheets or developing long-term business plans.

"Yeah, but there's still something more nagging at Mari. I heard her talking to Dad about a growing drug problem in the county. One that's affecting the clinic.''

Cecilia nodded glumly. "It's something we're all becoming concerned about. Controlled substances—especially powerful and addictive painkillers such as Orcadol—have become increasingly available through the black market here in the county. We're seeing an increase in drug-addicted mothers and in delivery complications. The number of stillbirths is up, as well as other infant medical problems. It seems as though the crisis has been intensifying during the past few months, particularly. I know Detective Collins has been hanging around a lot lately, trying to track down where the women are getting the drugs.''

"Well, that would certainly explain part of Mari's bad mood. I don't know if you're aware that she and

Bryce Collins were pretty seriously involved at one time. They broke up when he tried to force her to choose between him and the career in medicine she had always dreamed of. Fortunately, in my opinion, she chose medicine. Their breakup was unpleasant and painful, and they've hardly been on the best of terms since. In fact, Collins is pretty much a jerk about the whole thing. Even after all this time, he's still bitter and angry with Mari. If I find out he's been giving her trouble—''

''I really wouldn't know,'' Cecilia said hastily. ''I stay so busy and focused with my patients that I tend to fall out of the loop when it comes to any other department. I'm always the last to hear any official news—or even run-of-the-mill gossip—which is rather ironic, considering that my brother is a rising executive in the corporation.''

''And I'm usually in some other city, so I'm hardly in the loop myself. But I could tell that both Mari and Dad are completely preoccupied with business right now. In Dad's case I think it has something to do with the new public relations director.''

''Lillith Cunningham? I haven't met her yet, but I've heard she's nice.''

''I like her, and I know Mari's very fond of her. Dad seems to think she's a little kooky. He's very skeptical of some of her ideas. I hope he doesn't make things too difficult for her.''

''Your father seems like a very reasonable and practical man who puts the best interests of the company first.''

''You can say that again. Especially since my

mother died, my father lives and breathes Bingham Enterprises.''

''My brother was coming very close to doing the same thing. I've nagged him for ages about finding a balance between work and a personal life. Fortunately, I think Hannah and the baby will take care of that. He'll always be a dedicated employee, but now he'll have more in his life. As it should be.''

''This from the woman who just admitted she's so focused on her work she doesn't even keep up with office gossip?''

She smiled wryly. ''True. But don't forget I'm working on changing that.''

''I've hardly forgotten. And speaking of working on our little project...'' He shifted so smoothly that she found herself on her back beneath him almost before she realized his intentions.

Her weariness suddenly evaporated. Smiling up at him, she slid her arms around his neck. ''Does this mean you've recovered your energy?''

''I do believe I have.''

Pulling his mouth down to hers, she smiled against his lips. ''Strangely enough, so have I.''

The echoes of their groans of satisfaction had barely faded away when Geoff spoke into the darkness of Cecilia's bedroom a long time later. His voice was still gravelly. ''Cecilia?''

She couldn't seem to find the strength to form coherent words. ''Mmm?''

''Our baby's going to be beautiful.''

Melting into his arms, she smiled mistily into his damp shoulder. She had no doubt that Geoff was right—as he claimed to always be.

Chapter Eight

"Your suspicions were correct, Mrs. Hoover. You are definitely pregnant."

The thirty-six-year-old African-American woman sitting at the end of an exam table broke into a tearful smile in response to Cecilia's announcement. "I can't believe it. We've been trying for so long. And now to find out we've been successful…"

Her husband, a tall, lanky laborer in his early forties, looked torn between elation and trepidation. "How long till we can stop worrying about something going wrong?"

Because she knew Rebecca Hoover had suffered two miscarriages in the past, followed by several years of being unable to conceive, Cecilia understood his anxiety. "I can't offer any guarantees, of course, but everything looks good so far. I'll be working very closely with Dr. Kyle Bingham, who's an excellent pediatrician. We're going to monitor both your wife and the baby very closely, and do everything we can to make sure we deliver a healthy child in about seven months.''

She spent the next fifteen minutes outlining the plan of action for those next seven months. They talked about nutrition, vitamins and a checkup schedule, and then touched on some areas they would discuss in more detail later. By the time they left, the Hoovers seemed a bit calmer and determined to do everything within their power to make this pregnancy a successful one.

They had a tense few weeks ahead of them, Cecilia mused as she made some quick notes in Mrs. Hoover's file. As she had said, there were no guarantees, but she had a good feeling about this pregnancy. Of course, there was always a chance of complication when a first-time mother was over thirty-five.

Mrs. Hoover was a year younger than Cecilia.

Nervously moistening her lips, she closed the file. She was healthy, she assured herself. She ate well, took vitamins, exercised regularly. It was practically commonplace in some areas these days for women to wait until their late thirties and early forties to bear children. There was no reason at all to think she couldn't successfully conceive and carry a child. And considering Geoff's youth and fitness and, er, stamina, she couldn't imagine any problems in that respect.

It was sometimes still mind-boggling to her that she thought of him so casually—and so intimately. Considering that she had only met the man a few days ago, events were moving almost faster than she could comprehend. It was exciting but, to be honest, rather terrifying.

"Hey, Cecilia, I'm starving. Got time for lunch?" Vanessa had poked her head in the exam room to ask the question, big earrings swaying.

"Yeah, sure. I've got a half hour till my next appointment. Did you brown bag?"

"Tuna salad on a croissant. How about you?"

"Turkey on whole wheat." Standing, Cecilia moved toward the door. "And strawberry yogurt for dessert."

"Wanna trade? I've got chocolate-chip cookies."

Chuckling, Cecilia shook her head. "Thanks, but I'll stick with the yogurt."

She needed the calcium, a consideration she saw no need to mention since she didn't intend to go into further explanations. There would be time enough to fill Vanessa in when a pregnancy test produced a positive result. It wasn't going to be easy, since Vanessa was going to have a zillion questions, but of all Cecilia's friends and acquaintances, she knew Vanessa would be the most accepting.

Of course, Eric would support her decision, too, she assured herself. She had no doubt that he would be a loving and visible uncle for her child. But that wouldn't stop him from expressing his opinion about her decision to have a baby—specifically, Geoff Bingham's baby—without discussing the idea with him first.

Because Vanessa was pretty much in the very center of the loop when it came to workplace gossip, it shouldn't have surprised Cecilia at all when her friend said, "Tell me what's going on between you and Geoff Bingham."

They had just settled at a comfortable table for two in the atrium, a table tucked cozily into a plant-filled corner that offered some conversational privacy. Cecilia had barely had time to unwrap her sandwich. She set it down rather abruptly, not sure she could swallow just then. "What do you mean?"

"I know you had dinner with him after the reception Friday. A group of nursing students went to Melinda's that evening and they saw the two of you together. It was all over the clinic the next day."

Which explained how Eric had heard about it. It said something about Cecilia's absorption with Geoff that evening that she hadn't even seen the nursing students, though she'd recognized several other Melinda's patrons. She gave Vanessa the same vague explanation she had offered her brother. "We were both hungry, so we decided to have dinner together."

"And the movie last night?"

"You heard about that, too?"

"Honey, you delivered a baby in the movie theater, with Geoff Bingham's assistance. Did you think I *wouldn't* hear about it?"

Cecilia hadn't been quite that deeply into denial. The ambulance personnel had recognized both her and Geoff, of course, and the young parents, who had been brought to this hospital, had certainly known the names of the couple who had delivered their child.

Cecilia had been fielding questions and congratulations about the delivery all day—even being called for comment by a reporter for the local newspaper, the *Merlyn Mage*. She had given few details to the reporter, claiming client confidentiality as a hasty excuse to keep herself out of the headlines, but she knew there would be an article about the movie theater "premiere." Especially since Geoff Bingham had been involved.

"So...two dates with Geoff in one weekend. Sounds promising."

"We aren't dating, exactly."

"Oh. What *are* you doing?"

Cecilia focused very hard on the soda can in front of her. "Just hanging out. He's out of town so much he hardly knows anyone around here anymore. We enjoy each other's company because there's no real pressure. He's not trying to raise money from me—because, of course, I have none to donate—and I get a chance to spend a few pleasant evenings with someone who's only peripherally involved with the clinic, so there's very little shop talk."

Vanessa seemed downright disappointed by the practically of her friend's explanation. "Sounds pleasant. What a shame."

Cecilia smiled and shook her head, relieved that Vanessa's curiosity seemed somewhat appeased, but knowing she was going to have a lot of explaining to do eventually.

"So what's he like?"

"Geoff?" Cecilia picked up her sandwich again. "He's very nice. Charming, actually. Eric described him as the family politician, which sums him up pretty well, I suppose."

"So, you don't see a chance of anything long-term developing between you?"

Other than parenthood, no. But Cecilia said

merely, "If you're talking about marriage, all I can say is be serious. We couldn't be any more different. Besides, he'll be taking off again in a few weeks—Boston and then London, I think he said—and I have a very busy life right here."

Vanessa swallowed a bit of tuna salad sandwich, washing it down with a sip of bottled water. "Might as well take advantage of his company while he's here. How often do you have a chance to spend time with a gorgeous, rich young stud?"

"Not very often—obviously."

"So, how is it? In general, I mean."

Cecilia felt a stupid grin spread across her face. "All in all—it's great."

Vanessa sighed dramatically. "Just as I suspected. Oh, well, we old married ladies just have to be content with fantasizing."

"As if you'd rather have anyone other than George."

At the mention of her pudgy, balding and incredibly sweet husband, Vanessa giggled. "True. But that doesn't stop me from daydreaming about Denzel Washington occasionally. The occasional romantic fantasy never hurt any woman."

Cecilia supposed that was true—as long as the woman never let herself get so carried away with the daydream that she lost sight of the difference between fantasy and reality.

She was relieved when Vanessa was suddenly distracted. "Look, there's Detective Collins snooping around again. I hear he's been asking an awful lot of questions about our security protocols for controlled substances."

"The Orcadol epidemic again. He seems convinced he's going to find some leads here."

"I don't know, something about the way he's been skulking around here is starting to get my back up. Especially the way he watches Mari—as if he thinks she's deliberately interfering with his investigation or something. Just because she's too busy to be at his beck and call...."

A discussion about the drug crisis ensued, both Vanessa and Cecilia expressing concern about the toll it was taking on the young people in a community already burdened with poverty and illiteracy. By the time they had discussed several ideas for combating the problem through public awareness campaigns, they had finished their respective sandwiches and had to get back to work.

Determined to put thoughts of Geoff out of her mind—or at least, push them to the back of her thoughts—Cecilia headed for the examining rooms to visit with yet another expectant mother.

Geoff was having a bit of trouble concentrating on his work. He had no difficulty pinpointing the source of his distraction. The image of Cecilia Mendoza's pretty smile was too clear in his mind to leave him in any doubt.

Remembering the state of exhaustion he'd been in when he'd finally left her house last night, he chuckled and shook his head. He wasn't at all sure he would survive the next couple of weeks, but as the old saying went, at least he would go out with a smile on his face.

A disembodied voice came from a speaker on his

rarely used desk. "Mr. Bingham, your father is on line two."

He lifted the receiver to his ear. "Hey, Dad. What's up?"

Ron Bingham's voice was a rich baritone that suited his distinguished appearance. Still trim and fit at fifty-four, he had a full head of salt-and-pepper hair and a neatly trimmed beard and mustache. Geoff had been told for as long as he could remember that he had inherited his father's clear hazel eyes.

"I thought maybe you would like to have lunch today. Seems like you and I have hardly had a chance to see each other except in passing or in a crowd since you got into town."

There was a restless tone in Ron's voice that Geoff had been hearing more frequently lately. As Mari and Geoff became busier and more involved in their own lives, giving them less time to spend with their father, and as Ron passed over more of the responsibilities of running the family business to his offspring, Geoff wondered if Ron was feeling a bit at a loss.

Ron had always planned to retire with his beloved wife—leaving them free to travel and work in their spectacular gardens and continue their community activities. Violet's untimely death had left her grieving widower to face a future alone, and he made sure to grumble at every opportunity about the lack of grandchildren to spoil in his spare time.

Geoff had no doubt that Ron would be delighted to welcome Geoff's child into the family, especially once he recovered from the shock and skepticism. In fact, Geoff thought his father would be delighted with

Cecilia as the grandchild's mother if Ron had a chance to spend some time getting to know her.

Thinking it would have been nice if she could have joined them for lunch, Geoff said, "Sure, Dad. Lunch sounds good. I haven't had a chance to look up all day and I could use the break."

"Great. We can catch up. You can tell me when you found time to sneak into midwifery classes."

"When I did what? Oh. You heard about the theater incident."

"Yes. I heard you helped deliver a strapping baby boy. Nice job, son, but must you take business from our clinic?"

"Trust me, I'd have been delighted to send her to the clinic. But her baby apparently has a thing for action films. Kid's probably going to be a stunt man or something."

Ron laughed. "I can't wait to hear all the details. Including how you ended up being at the theater with Eric Mendoza's sister. I didn't even know you two were acquainted."

Geoff was already planning a carefully edited description of his friendship with Cecilia when he hung up the phone with a promise to meet his father in half an hour.

It was after 7:00 p.m. by the time Cecilia climbed out of her car that evening. Geoff had some sort of meeting with investors that night, so they wouldn't be seeing each other.

She should probably be looking forward to an evening alone to read and catch up on some chores around her house. She wasn't usually the type to want

to spend every evening doing something or seeing people. Usually, after a long day of dealing with people at the clinic, she was perfectly content to spend a few hours in peaceful solitude.

She had just unlocked her door when a commotion from next door made her pause. She could hear Brandy's voice, shrilly raised in anger, and then the slamming of her neighbors' back door.

Another fight between Brandy and her grandparents, Cecilia thought with a sigh. Probably about Marlin again. It was Brandy's custom to sulk in her grandparents' backyard after one of those confrontations. Sometimes Cecilia went out to talk to her, trying to calm her and help her see the older generation's side of things.

Tonight she really just wanted to close herself into her own house and pretend she hadn't heard anything. After all, she had her own problems to think about. Brandy would probably rather Cecilia mind her own business, anyway.

And then, hearing an angry sob coming from the neighbors' backyard, Cecilia sighed. She would go inside and put up her purse, then see if there was anything she could do to help Brandy.

Poor Maxine, Cecilia thought as she stepped into her house. It had been difficult for the older woman to become a mother again after so many years. Especially since Brandy had been raised so haphazardly, resulting in a teenager who was bright and articulate but often rebellious and defiant.

She had just set her purse down when her telephone rang. Tempted to let the machine pick up, she decided instead to answer, just in case it was an important call. "Hello?"

"How was your day?"

Just the sound of Geoff's deep voice made some of the tension seep from her muscles. She felt a smile replace the worried frown her neighbors' problems had caused. "Long. Busy. But not bad. How was yours?"

"You just summed mine up pretty well. Long. Busy. Not bad."

"I thought you had a business thing tonight."

"Yeah. It starts at eight. I was just trying to work up some enthusiasm for the event."

"From the expression in your voice, I take it you're having a hard time doing so."

"Impossible. Can't stand a couple of the jerks I'll be dining with. But that doesn't mean I won't be on my best behavior while I try to convince them that fertility research is a worthy cause for their charitable donations. And somehow convince them that the crazy rumors about the most controversial plans Mari has on her agenda are mostly just that—rumors. I wish I could figure out who's spreading all the talk about Mari lately. We Binghams have always been targeted for gossip—some admittedly legitimate but much of it spurred by petty jealousies—but, from what little I've heard since I've been in town, it seems particularly vicious lately."

"Poor Mari. She looked so tired and worried when I saw her this afternoon. I admire your sister a great deal, Geoff. I'm sorry she's going through such a difficult time."

"I know she would appreciate your concern."

"If only Detective Collins could make some headway with his investigation so he would stop getting underfoot. At least that would be one annoyance off Mari's shoulders."

"Maybe I should have a little discussion with Detective Collins," Geoff growled.

"He is conducting an official investigation, Geoff. And there really is a serious drug problem in Merlyn County. We had another addicted pregnant woman come in today with serious medical complications. As annoyingly persistent as the detective is, I hope his efforts will pay off by cutting the supply of black market drugs that are wreaking so much havoc on our community."

"You're right," Geoff conceded reluctantly. "I shouldn't let my personal bias against Mari's ex-boyfriend interfere with necessary police business. I just wish he could do his work without causing Mari so much stress."

"Yes, so do I."

"Do you have any big plans for the evening?"

Cecilia thought of the teenager sobbing so angrily next door. The crisis that was none of her business, actually, but in which she felt obligated to get involved. "No. No big plans."

"I envy you. Actually, I'd like to be there with you. We could have a nice, quiet pizza-and-television night. Or I could bring my guitar and serenade you."

"You play guitar?"

"Contrary to what my sister might tell you, yes, I do play guitar. Mostly oldies—Beatles tunes, especially. My mother was a Beatles fanatic. Other kids heard lullabies at bedtime, I heard 'Hey, Jude.'"

"What about 'Golden Slumbers'? That's a Beatles tune that makes a very nice lullaby."

"You're a Beatles fan?"

"Of course. They were brilliant songwriters and musicians. 'Norwegian Wood' is one of my all-time favorite melodies."

"And one of my favorite songs to play."

"Then you'll definitely have to play it for me."

"A woman after my own heart. And, yes, I know," he added, laughing. "You aren't after anyone's heart. But I still think you're very cool."

She was cool, Cecilia thought as she hung up the phone a few moments later when Geoff reluctantly disconnected so he could prepare for his business meeting. It wasn't exactly a flowery or poetic compliment—and he had definitely been speaking tongue-in-cheek—but still she found herself beaming with pleasure.

She really wasn't after Geoff's heart, she assured herself, but she suspected he had already taken over a little corner of hers.

Cecilia rarely took an entire day off work, but she had scheduled Tuesday as a stay-at-home day. She had accumulated two weeks' vacation from the clinic, and she preferred taking it a day or two at a time rather than all at once. With the support of her supervisors, she had arranged her summer schedule so that she wouldn't be away from her patients for very long, yet would still have periodic breaks.

Though she had made no secret of her plans for the day, even mentioning them to Geoff, she wasn't expecting company Tuesday morning. It was with both surprise and curiosity that she heard what sounded like a motorcycle pulling into her driveway, followed by the musical peal of her doorbell.

Climbing down from a stepladder in the tiny front bedroom of her house, she automatically smoothed a hand down her hot-pink T-shirt and denim shorts. Her hair was up in a loose ponytail, and she had applied just a touch of makeup that morning—a habit too strong to break even when she planned a day at home alone. Could this be a delivery of some sort? She wasn't expecting anything, but she supposed it was possible.

Checking the security window before unlocking the door, she reached quickly for the dead bolt. "Geoff," she said a moment later. "What are you doing here?"

He smiled, and she had a moment to reflect on how unfair it was that he could look so breathtakingly handsome even with his hair all tumbled and wearing a plain gray T-shirt, faded, worn jeans and scuffed boots. "You said you were going to spend the day doing home maintenance projects. Since I didn't have any pressing business, I thought I'd give you a hand, if that's okay with you. I'd have called first, but it was sort of an impulse."

She looked behind him toward the big black-and-chrome motorcycle sitting in her driveway, a black-and-silver helmet dangling from the handlebars. "You came on that?"

"Yeah. I don't get a chance to ride it much, and it needs to be taken out occasionally to keep it purring. Maybe you want to go for a ride later? I've got a second helmet strapped to the back."

"Er, uh, thanks, but I'll probably have to wash my hair or something this afternoon."

Geoff laughed. "You sound like my family. Don't tell me you're afraid of my bike."

"I'm just not really the motorcycle type."

"Maybe you'll give me a chance to change your mind about that."

Cecilia truly doubted that was going to happen. She didn't even like the idea of Geoff careening around on that dangerous-looking machine. Pushing some painful old memories to the back of her mind, she held the door wider.

"Come in," she said, turning her back on the motorcycle. "Can I get you anything?"

"I didn't come to be entertained." He closed the door behind him. "I came to work. What's on the agenda?"

"Painting. I just finished taping off the front bedroom."

"Painting, huh?" He looked momentarily doubtful, then nodded. "Okay, lead me to it."

Planting her hands on her hips, Cecilia tilted her head to study him. "Have you ever actually painted a room before?"

"I scribbled on my bedroom wall with felt-tip markers when I was five. I thought it looked pretty good myself, but my mother wasn't as enthusiastic about it."

She couldn't help laughing. "You must have been a handful."

"Actually, I was a model child. I just indulged in small rebellions every once in a while."

"I think you still indulge in the occasional rebellion,'' she murmured, thinking of the motorcycle. Not to mention his present arrangement with her.

"Me? Nah. I'm still a model child."

Smiling, she took his arm and tugged slightly. "Come on, I'll show you how to paint a room the proper way."

He put a hand on her wrist and tugged her into his arms, covering her mouth with his for a long, hungry kiss. She was practically panting by the time it ended.

"Now," he said, looking rather proud of himself, "I'm ready to learn how to paint."

After that mind-emptying kiss, Cecilia just hoped she remembered how.

Chapter Nine

Geoff followed Cecilia down her hallway at a bit of a distance. He liked watching her walk, her slender legs nicely showcased by her denim shorts. She glanced over her shoulder, caught him watching her, and gave him a look. Totally unrepentant, he grinned back at her.

The room she led him into was small, no more than ten by ten. She had taken out all the furniture, if there had been any to start with. The windows and base-boards had all been carefully outlined with blue masking tape. Plastic sheeting covered the wood floor. A bucket of paint sat in the center of the room next to a paint tray, a couple of rollers and some brushes in assorted sizes. "Looks like you know what you're doing."

"I've done a lot of painting. I can't afford to hire

someone to do something I'm perfectly capable of doing myself. Eric offered to help next weekend, but this room's so small, it won't really take long. If there's anything else you would rather be doing, I can handle this alone.''

"Nope. There's not a thing I would rather be doing than painting this room.''

"You expect me to believe that?''

"Okay, maybe there is one thing I'd rather be doing. But since you're busy in here, I suppose that will have to wait.''

He liked it when she gave him those dryly chiding looks. Which must be why he kept doing or saying things to earn them. "So what color are we painting?'' he asked before she could come up with a response to his entendre. "The same off white that's in here now?''

"No.'' She bent to remove the lid from the can, revealing the pale green paint inside.

Not quite a pastel, he decided. More of a soft, moss green. "Nice.''

"I was thinking this would be a good color for a…well, for a nursery. I like something different than the usual pinks, blues and yellows.''

"A nursery.'' Geoff reached up to massage the back of his neck as he looked around the room again from this new perspective. "Uh, yeah, green's nice.''

She seemed to be staring rather fiercely at the paint. "I know I'm getting a little ahead of myself, but the room needs to be painted, anyway, and this is a color that will work just as well in a guest room if we don't—well, if our plans don't work out. If they do,

I thought I would use light maple woods with green, butterscotch and cream accents for the nursery.''

"I would have thought you'd prefer bold, primary colors.''

"Because of the rest of my house, you mean? I admit, I do have a weakness for bold colors, but I think a nursery should be relaxing. Peaceful. And the earthy colors I have in mind should create that effect.'' She straightened abruptly. "Not that you're at all interested in my decorating plans. Really, Geoff, if you would rather go ride your motorcycle, I—''

"Cecilia.'' He rested a hand on her arm. "I'm interested. Let me help.''

Her smile was tentative. "I'd like that.''

Brushing a kiss across her lips, he drew back and glanced again around the room, picturing a maple crib against the far wall. "Where do we start?''

Cecilia picked up a paint roller and held it out to him. "That paint goes on these walls. It's a fairly simple process. Try not to get it on your clothes.''

It was fairly simple, actually. And unexpectedly pleasant. Working side by side with Cecilia, rolling paint on the walls of the room that might one day hold their child. Sharing warm smiles, talking about inconsequential matters. Stopping for the occasional stolen kiss.

It was nice. Almost…domestic, he thought, and promptly dropped the paintbrush he had been wielding for a few finishing touches. Paint splattered his jeans and his right boot, then puddled beneath the brush on the plastic sheeting. "Great.''

"Oh, my. You made a mess.'' Cecilia was obviously making an effort not to laugh at him.

"Yes, I did."

"Fortunately, the paint washes off with soap and water. I don't think it will stain your jeans if you launder them quickly."

"What about skin? Does it wash off skin with soap and water?"

"Yes. Why? Did you get paint on your—Geoff!" She stared in disbelief at the paint he had just smeared on her arm with his fingertip. "Why did you do that?"

"Call it an impulse." It must have been the same impulse that made him reach out and place a dot of paint on the tip of her very cute nose.

She reached up to slap his hand. "Have you lost your mind?"

"Sorry." He rested a hand on her cheek. Since he had just deliberately squeezed the bristles of the wet paintbrush, he left a perfect green print on her smooth skin. "Sometimes I just can't help myself."

Her chocolate-brown eyes were huge. "Um, did you just leave paint on my face?"

"Yes. And green is definitely your color."

"I cannot believe you did that."

"Well, since I got paint all over me...."

"But *I* didn't put it there."

"That's true. I suppose I owe you an apology."

"Apology accepted." She patted his cheek, leaving a wet, sticky residue behind. "You know, actually, green looks quite good on you, too."

He laughed. "Oh, lady, are you in trouble now."

"Don't even think about—"

Before she could finish the sentence, he had her on her back and on the floor, plastic sheeting crinkling beneath her. Laughing, she squirmed beneath him as he tickled her with scattered kisses and neck nuzzles. "You crazy man," she said in gasps. "This is *not* the way to paint a room."

"I think it's a great way to paint a room." He kissed her again, fancying that he could taste her sweet smile. With maybe a slight hint of paint thrown in, he thought, grinning against her lips.

The humor carried them out of the guest room/nursery into Cecilia's bedroom. They were still playing and laughing when they stepped into the shower to wash off the paint. But as the warm water cascaded over them and their soapy hands began to wander, the laughter and banter faded.

He crowded her against the tiles, dipping his head to cover her mouth with his. She was so small, delicately boned, yet strong and capable. As comfortable climbing a ladder as she was cradling a fragile newborn in her arms. What man wouldn't want a woman like this to be the mother of his children?

Oops. Wrong word. Children implied a long-term commitment, not a one-time partnership.

Deciding not to think beyond this day—not even beyond this moment—he pulled her closer. Her arms went around him, and it pleased him that she seemed as eager to be close to him as he was to be close to her.

Their wet bodies fused. The kiss went deeper. Became almost hot enough to cause the shower water to steam around them. He lifted her against the wall, bringing her mouth within easier reach, and she wrapped her legs around him.

Humor had been completely replaced now with

hunger. His need was so great his knees were weak with it, forcing him to brace Cecilia against the shower wall.

He wanted her. Desperately. It had nothing at all to do just then with any agreements or plans they had made, but everything to do with her warm smiles, her beautiful eyes, her generous heart and dry sense of humor. The only goal he had in mind just then was mutual satisfaction. And in that quest Cecilia seemed to be a very willing partner.

"Are you sure you won't take a ride with me?"

Cecilia looked over her shoulder for a moment to answer, drawing her attention away from the last of the painting supplies she had been cleaning. "I'm absolutely certain. But promise me you'll be careful on that thing."

He smiled and leaned over to kiss the tip of her nose, which was now scrubbed free of paint. "Careful is my middle name."

"Yeah, right," she muttered, thinking of their exploits in the spare room. And in the shower. And then in her bed.

"You'd better put those clothes in the wash as soon as you get home—or have your maid or housekeeper or whoever take care of them," she added, suddenly doubting that Geoff Bingham did his own laundry. "As it is, I'm going to be scrubbing paint out of my shorts for a while—thanks to your roving hands."

He looked more proud of himself than apologetic. "If those shorts are ruined, I'll buy you another pair. Heck, I'll buy you a dozen. That will give me a chance to ruin a few more with my, er, roving hands.''

She found it hard to hold on to her smile when he talked about buying her anything. Even though she knew he was joking, reminders of the difference in their financial standing didn't strike her as particularly funny.

He stepped up behind her and kissed the back of her neck, which she had bared by pinning her damp hair into a loose roll. ''Any other chores I can help you do around here?''

She wasn't sure she would survive any more of his help. ''No, thank you. You didn't have to work today?''

Helping himself to an apple sitting in a bowl on the counter, Geoff shook his head. ''I've decided I deserve an occasional day off, myself. After all, I worked until late last night, if you count a business dinner as work, which I do.''

Cecilia wiped her hands on a paper towel and reached for the teakettle, deciding she would prepare herself a cup of herbal tea. She was making a deliberate effort to cut back on coffee, which would be good for her health—and for the child she hoped to carry. ''How did it go last night?''

''Not bad. Maybe we soothed a few concerns about some of the craziest rumors buzzing around. I've got to admit Lillith Cunningham did a good job working the crowd. Not that you'd get my dad to admit that.''

''He's still resisting her?''

''He still thinks her ideas are too impractical. She's talking now about using my grandmother as a spokeswoman for the medical facilities. He thinks that's just foolish.''

Cecilia took a moment to think about that idea. ''Actually, that's not a bad suggestion. No one would be a more knowledgeable or passionate spokesperson than Myrtle Bingham. After all, she's the one who founded the Janice Foster Memorial Midwifery Clinic and Women's Health Center. And she's obviously the perfect representative for the Myrtle Northrup Bingham School of Midwifery. Who better to talk about the need for readily available quality prenatal and delivery facilities?''

Geoff swallowed a bite of apple. ''Actually, I thought it was an idea with potential, myself. If my grandmother wants to take that on, I'd say more power to her. She's still healthy and vibrant and sharp as a tack, and I've always believed that staying active goes a long way toward keeping her that way.''

''So what's your father's objection?''

''I'm not sure, exactly. Lillith just seems to rub him the wrong way.''

''Odd. Do you want a cup of tea?''

''Do you have any juice?''

''In the fridge. Help yourself.''

Geoff opened the refrigerator and pulled out a bottle of grape juice. As he poured it into a glass, he said, ''You know, I was thinking....''

''Always a frightening prospect,'' Cecilia murmured, dunking a tea bag into a mug of boiling water.

He grinned. ''Smart aléc. Anyway, what do you thinking about joining my family for dinner tomorrow night? Grandmother's having us at her house.''

Her hand froze in the process of stirring her tea.

Dinner with Geoff's family? "Thank you, but I think I'd better pass."

Leaning against the counter, he lowered his glass to look at her. "Why?"

"I just think it would be...awkward. You haven't told anyone what we're trying to do, have you?"

"No, of course not. That's strictly between us, for now. I just thought you might enjoy spending an evening with my family. I know they would enjoy your company."

"If you don't mind, I'd rather not this time. I actually have a couple of things to do tomorrow evening at the clinic. I'm helping out with a Lamaze class, and there's always a ton of paperwork to catch up on."

He didn't look particularly satisfied by her decision, but he didn't push. Probably because he knew it wouldn't have done any good. "All right. Maybe some other time before I leave town."

She didn't want to think about him leaving town. Or about spending an evening with his father, sister and grandmother, who would be bound to wonder what was going on between the midwife and their fair-haired boy.

Thoughts of Geoff didn't actually interfere with Cecilia's work on Wednesday. But they stayed very close to the front of her mind all day as she saw patient after patient in her regular, busy appointment schedule.

She'd had such a wonderful day with Geoff on Tuesday. Who would have thought she could have so much fun painting a room?

"You've dilated to two centimeters, Angie. I wouldn't be at all surprised if we see that baby by the end of the day tomorrow."

"I sure hope so. My back is killin' me."

Geoff had hung around for the remainder of Tuesday evening, and they had indulged in the pizza-and-television quiet time he claimed to have been craving. She liked veggie pizzas and he preferred pepperoni, so they'd ordered a half-and-half. She liked watching the home and garden channel and he preferred the news channels, but it turned out they both liked the history channel, so they'd found an interesting documentary there that they had both enjoyed.

Funny how well they had gotten along from the beginning, she mused. There seemed to be no silent competition between them, no need for them to have their own ways or prove they were right. That was more than she had ever accomplished with her ex-husband, who saw every disagreement as a challenge he had to win.

"I'm very proud of you for giving up cigarettes for your baby's sake, Jolene. I know it's been hard for you, but your daughter will appreciate it."

"It has been hard, but when you told me all the bad things cigarette smoke could do to my baby, I knew I had to quit. Low birth weight, developmental disorders, asthma and other respiratory complications—I couldn't live with any of those possibilities. I've known for a long time that I should quit, but my baby gave me the best reason to finally do it."

"The important thing is, you made your health and that of your unborn child's a priority, and I commend you for that. Stay strong, okay?"

"For my baby's sake, I will."

Parenthood involved sacrifice, and Cecilia was as prepared to make them as any of the eager mothers under her care. She sometimes had trouble identifying with the women who weren't willing to give up—or at least make the effort to give up—the bad habits that were detrimental to their unborn children.

This Orcadol crisis, for example. It simply broke her heart every time she came into contact with someone so deeply addicted that the drugs became more important than anything else.

Which was why she had mixed feelings about the impending confrontation that seemed to be building between the clinic director and the perhaps-over-zealous detective assigned to the Orcadol case. As much as Cecilia admired Mari Bingham, she hoped Mari's old, hard feelings toward Bryce Collins were not blinding her to the importance of his work. Cecilia knew how protective and defensive Mari was about the medical facilities she had devoted her entire life to, but if anyone here was involved with the black-market drug ring, the truth must be exposed.

It wasn't as if Bryce was accusing Mari of protecting drug pushers, after all. More likely their old wounds were preventing them from communicating effectively.

"So it's okay if I keep getting my hair dyed while I'm pregnant? I sure would hate to have to be half blond and half brunette for the next few months."

"Yes, Lacey, you may keep dying your hair as long as you let your hairdresser know to take reasonable precautions with ventilation. There's no medical evidence that hair dye causes any problems in pregnancy.''

"Man, I'm glad to hear that. It was hard enough having to give up drinking a beer at the bowling alley on Friday nights. But I'd have really hated to give up my hair dye.''

It had been a pretty good day so far, Cecilia mused as she moved on with a smile to the next patient. Busy, but not particularly difficult. As long as she concentrated on her work and not on her relationship—or whatever it could be called—with Geoff, she could function quite normally.

When she did steal a few moments to think of Geoff between tasks, she ended up staring into space, reliving a few special moments and dreaming of what might come....

She checked on a patient in a birthing room, still at least an hour away from delivery. There was a real party going on in that room, with the father, two grandmothers, a maternal aunt and an eager big sister all awaiting the birth. Comparing that scene to her first delivery that morning—a fourteen-year-old girl accompanied only by a rather detached foster mother—Cecilia thought about how the presence of a supportive and welcoming family made the whole process so much more joyous.

For the first time, it occurred to her that Geoff might want to be present when their child was born. He had made it clear enough that he intended to take an active role in his child's life. He was approaching parenthood the same way Cecilia was, which she could understand, but she couldn't help wondering how much more complicated his participation would make things for her. Especially when it came to *his* family....

She was still surprised that he had invited her to join him this evening at his grandmother's house for a family dinner. That was taking their partnership into sticky territory, as far as she was concerned. It would be much better to make explanations later, after they had accomplished their goal, than during the process. Not that they would tell anyone they were trying to have a baby, of course, but everyone would assume she was dating Geoff with another purpose in mind— maybe even marriage—and she didn't want to deal with that misconception.

Oddly enough, it seemed easier to explain a pregnancy resulting from a passing affair than to face speculation about why Geoff Bingham was spending so much of his rare time in town with her.

But it really had been nice of him to invite her, she reflected with a slight smile. Nice to think that he hadn't yet grown tired of her company.

"Cecilia, you're wanted in birthing room two. Looks like things are started to get underway in there."

"Thank you, Crystal." Trying to put her own concerns out of her mind for a while longer, Cecilia smiled at the younger woman and made an effort to penetrate the cloud of melancholy that seemed to surround Crystal these days. "How is Ryan, Crystal? Is he going to play T-ball this year?"

Usually, questions about her six-year-old son were guaranteed to bring a smile to Crystal's face. This time, her eyes looked instantly stricken, instead. She recovered quickly, masking her emotions behind the rather sullen expression she had been wearing lately, to the concern of many of her co-workers. "Ryan's with his father right now," she mumbled.

"Still? Oh, I thought…"

Cecilia could have sworn she saw a sheen of tears in the younger woman's eyes as Crystal turned abruptly away. "You'd better hurry to room two. Mrs. Vargas is anxious to see you."

Watching Crystal hurry away, her shoulders hunched, her posture unmistakably defensive, Cecilia decided that her associates had good reason to be concerned about the woman. Something was very definitely wrong there. Maybe she should talk to Vanessa, who had such a knack of dealing with the younger employees. Maybe Vanessa would have better luck with Crystal.

Pushing away the ever-present paperwork that would still be waiting for her after this much-anticipated baby made its debut, Cecilia also mentally pushed away her personal concerns. She had a job to do.

Cecilia had only been home for a few minutes that evening when her doorbell rang. It couldn't be Geoff, she thought with a puzzled frown. Tonight was his family dinner, and she thought she had made it clear that he couldn't change her mind about accompanying him.

Setting down the chicken breast she had been preparing to broil for her dinner, she hurried into the living room to answer the door.

A delivery truck sat in her driveway, and the driver

stood at the door, a pleasant smile gracing his florid face. "Cecilia Mendoza?"

"Yes?"

"I have a delivery for you. Would you sign here, please?"

"Yes, of course." She used the stylus he offered her to awkwardly sign her name on the electronic screen—a skill she had never quite mastered in her usual handwriting. She couldn't imagine what this delivery could be. It wasn't a flower truck, she thought, watching as the delivery driver opened the back of the vehicle.

The box was big enough to require a wheeled dolly. She watched in wide-eyed curiosity as the driver guided it onto her porch and through her front door. "Where would you like it? It's not particularly heavy, just awkward."

"Just leave it here in the living room. You're sure this is for me?"

He chuckled. "Yes, ma'am. Has your name and address written right here on this tag. Have a good evening, Ms. Mendoza."

"Thank you." Closing the door behind him, she turned to study the box for a moment. And then she ran to find a knife with which to slice through the wrapping tape.

Her heart jumped right into her throat when she saw the contents of the box. There was no card, but then, none was needed. She knew exactly who had sent this gift.

Fighting back a quick rush of tears, she ran an unsteady hand across the back of the small, beautiful maple rocker. The seat was covered with a gingham cushion in the exact shade of green she and Geoff had applied to the walls of the room she hoped would become a nursery. This rocker was absolutely perfect for holding a baby. And it was even made of the very wood she had said she wanted to use.

He really shouldn't have done this, she thought, unable to resist sinking into the cushioned seat and rocking a little. It was such an extravagant, unexpected gesture. One that could make her fall entirely too hard for him. The kind that could endanger the carefully objective perspective she was trying to maintain during their temporary affair.

They didn't even know that their efforts would be successful. Though there was no medical reason that she knew of preventing her from conceiving, there was still a very strong chance that these three weeks of effort would be fruitless, and who knew when—or if—they would try again. The disappointment of that would be bad enough, but it was going to be even worse if she was foolish enough to let her heart get broken in the process.

Chapter Ten

Geoff had tried not to mind when Cecilia turned down his dinner-with-the-family invitation. She'd been afraid it would be awkward, but he really didn't agree with that fear.

She already knew his family, at least in passing. Because of the clinic, they had plenty of topics for conversation. It wasn't completely unprecedented for him to bring a date to dinner, though admittedly it had been a while. No one would have wondered why he'd be interested in spending time with an attractive, interesting woman while he was in town.

It certainly would have saved him the ordeal of having his grandmother fixing him up with a lovely young woman who was the granddaughter of one of Myrtle's ladies-who-lunch friends. Although Myrtle had enthusiastically described the twenty-six-year-old attorney as a paragon of modern young woman-hood—beautiful, intelligent, ambitious and person-able—Geoff had no interest in meeting her, much to his grandmother's exasperation.

"I'm not going to be in town much longer, any-way," he had reminded her. "I leave for Boston in less than a month."

"But you'll be back. And as you take over more of your father's responsibilities, you'll be staying in town more." She was as quick with a retort as al-ways. "It is time for you to think about starting your family while you're young enough to enjoy them, Geoffrey. And while your father and I are around to enjoy them, too," she had added with a shake of her finger.

Geoff had chuckled and kissed his grandmother's softly lined cheek. "Emotional blackmail doesn't work with me, you should know that. And besides, you're going to be around for a long time yet."

The truth was, he thought as he drove his car into Cecilia's driveway Thursday evening, he simply wasn't interested in meeting his grandmother's friend's granddaughter. For the usual reasons, yes. No inclination to get caught up in a matchmaking scheme that would only lead to bruised feelings all around when he failed to cooperate. That same old reluctance to sacrifice any of his cherished freedom.

But there was another reason that he didn't care about meeting the single lawyer. He was enjoying Ce-cilia's company so much that he didn't want anything to interfere with their time together.

Holding a small package in his hand, he climbed out of his car with a smile on his face that was becoming increasingly familiar whenever he was about to see Cecilia. The smile turned to a frown when he heard a rather disturbing commotion coming from the house next door.

He glanced instinctively that way, spotting the rusty pickup he'd seen before parked in front of the house. Though overgrown shrubbery prevented him from seeing anyone on the shadowy porch, the voices were coming from there.

They sounded young. A male who was obviously angry—irate, even. And a girl who seemed to be speaking in sobs. He remembered the redhead with the bruised face that he had seen with Cecilia. Brandy? The one Cecilia had explained was being raised by her grandparents next door.

Were the grandparents home now? Were they aware that their granddaughter's boyfriend was throwing an obscenity-laced tantrum on their front porch?

A muffled thud might have been a blow, or a push followed by a fall. The sound was accompanied by a choked cry that made him toss the package he'd been holding onto the hood of his car and move purposefully toward the house next door.

Before he'd crossed Cecilia's lawn, a door slammed, and the battered pickup peeled out of the driveway, gunned so violently that the tires smoked on the asphalt. Brandy ran down the porch steps into Geoff's view, crying and calling after the departing truck. "Marlin, wait! Don't go, please!"

"Is there anything I can do to help?" Geoff asked her, raising his voice to be heard over her sobs.

She hadn't seen him prior to his speaking. She jumped and whirled toward him.

Her face was red and tear streaked, her eyes wild beneath her tumbled red hair. "What?"

"Is there anything I can do for you?"

"No." She swiped at her streaming eyes with the back of one hand, calling his attention to the fading bruise on her cheek.

Softball injury? He seriously doubted it. "Look, Brandy, I heard that lot yelling at you—"

"It was my fault," she said quickly, defensively. "I said some things that made him mad. He's got a quick temper, but he's not a bad guy."

He suspected that he would accomplish nothing by verbally attacking her jerk of a boyfriend. "Are your grandparents home?"

"No." Drawing a ragged breath, Brandy turned dispiritedly toward the door. "I'll be okay. I'm going in to wait for Marlin to call. He'll calm down pretty soon, and he'll be sorry he yelled at me like that. He's really a great guy. I love him a lot."

He wished he could think of something profound to say. Some wise words to get through her infatuated defensiveness and bring her to her senses. But all he could think of was, "Brandy, no one has the right to curse at you like that. And he damned sure doesn't have a right to put his hands on you in anger. If he has hit you, or shoved you—"

"You don't even know him!" Brandy snapped, hunching her skinny shoulders in an unmistakably closed posture. "Just leave me alone, okay?"

Sighing, Geoff held up both hands and stepped

back, signaling surrender. He watched as Brandy ran up the steps into her grandparents' house.

Okay, he'd blown that big-time, he thought in disgust. Instead of convincing Brandy to give Marlin the boot, he had probably sent her right back into his abusive arms.

Maybe Cecilia would have a better idea of what to do. He turned back toward her house, remembering to retrieve the package from the hood of his car.

In response to his knock, Cecilia opened the door with a smile that went a long way toward restoring his good mood. And then she pulled him inside, tugged his head down to hers, and gave him a kiss that nearly fried his brain circuitry. There wasn't an inch of him that wasn't hard by the time they finally broke apart for oxygen.

"What—" His voice cracked, and he had to stop to clear it before continuing. "What was that for?"

"For the rocker," she said, her eyes glowing as she smiled up at him.

"You already thanked me for the rocker, on the phone."

"Now you've been thanked in person."

"In person is definitely better," he murmured, and pulled her into his arms again.

He managed to end the kiss this time before it flared completely out of control. He was within a heartbeat of taking her right there on the entryway floor. His arms were around her, their bodies plastered together. He'd have sworn he was holding something else when he came in....

Clearing his thoughts with a slight shake of his head, he reached down to scoop up the package he had dropped sometime during the first kiss. "I forgot. I brought you something."

Suddenly she was frowning. "Another gift? Really, Geoff, that wasn't necessary. I mean, the rocker was already too much. You mustn't keep—"

"Maybe you should see what it is before you start fussing."

Looking decidedly wary, she accepted the bag and peered into it. And then she smiled and pulled out a small, colorful tin. "It's tea."

"Herbal. It's made of rose leaves and some other stuff from the garden that's supposed to taste good when you steep it all in boiling water. My grandmother loves it—and its caffeine free. Much better for you than all that coffee you drink."

Her smile was just a bit embarrassed by her automatic assumption that he had brought her something expensive. "It looks good. I'll try a cup tonight. Thank you."

"Something smells delicious."

"Dinner's almost ready."

"Need any help?"

"You can stand there and look pretty while I finish up."

"Very funny." But he was smiling when he followed her into the kitchen.

Cecilia had just set the food on the table when Geoff suddenly smacked his forehead with the heel of his hand. "I almost forgot."

"What?"

"Your neighbor. Brandy." He quickly told her what he had overheard when he'd arrived at her house. "Your, um, warm welcome sent it completely out of my head. She's over there by herself now, if you think you should check on her."

Concerned, Cecilia moved to the kitchen window and peered out. "Her grandparents must have just gotten home. I see their car in the carport now."

"Good. Then they can talk to her."

"Oh, they'll talk to her. They'll tell her what a loser Marlin is, and she'll get mad and yell back at them. Then she'll storm out to the backyard and sulk for a while. And tomorrow she'll be with Marlin again, letting him treat her like dirt because she has convinced herself he's her soul mate."

Geoff scowled. "I've got to tell you, Cecilia, I think the guy's doing worse than treating her badly. I think he's physically abusing her."

Her stomach muscles clenched. "You mean—"

"I mean, I don't believe for a minute that she was hit in the face by a softball. I think she was hit by a fist. And I'm pretty sure he either hit her or shoved her again tonight before I could get over there."

"Surely Brandy wouldn't keep excusing Marlin if he was actually hitting her."

"You haven't seen any other bruises or injuries?"

Cecilia thought about the question for a moment and then grimaced. "There have been a couple of bruises. And she sprained her wrist last month. She said she fell. But she's the active type who's always doing something physical like roller skating and climbing and swimming at the lake. I thought she was just a bit accident-prone."

She stopped and sighed. "I guess I wasn't really

thinking at all. If I had been, I would have recognized the signs.''

''From what I've read, abused women are very adept at hiding the truth from their friends and family. Covering, making excuses, taking the blame.''

Cecilia still felt like an idiot. ''I've seen it more than a few times in my job. You would be surprised and disgusted by the number of men who don't stop punching their wives or girlfriends even during pregnancy. And the women almost always have a cover story—running into a door or falling off a porch or, well, getting hit by a softball. Or if they're confronted by the truth, they make excuses for the jerks. The poor guy was just under stress or worried about money or being treated badly at work. Or maybe he'd had a little too much to drink and he wasn't really in control of his actions, but he's always so sorry later.''

''Brandy claimed this quarrel was all her fault. She said things she shouldn't have and Marlin got mad. She was obviously ready to crawl to keep him from leaving.''

''I just can't understand why she's so desperate to hang on to him. I've tried to convince her that she doesn't have to have a boyfriend to make her happy, but she has an almost neurotic fear of losing him.''

''From what you've told me of her background, she's looking for someone to belong to. Someone who puts her first. It's a shame she can't find that with her grandparents rather than with some boy who doesn't appreciate her.''

''I'll talk to her grandmother tomorrow. Maybe a family counselor can help them. And I'll try talking to Brandy again, though I'm not sure it would do any good. She thinks of me as her grandmother's unmarried neighbor. She likes me well enough, but she thinks I'm too old to understand teenage love affairs. Nor is she interested in modeling herself after me. According to her, my life is boring—all work and very little play, in her opinion. She doesn't understand when I tell her how much I love my work.''

"Maybe you should take her to work with you someday. Let her see what a vital and fascinating job you have.''

"If I thought it would accomplish anything, I would do that. But I'm not sure showing her my work would convince her that she should listen to me rather than Marlin.''

"It couldn't hurt for her to watch a woman who's competent, highly respected and fully in charge of vitally important situations.''

She couldn't help but be pleased, of course, by the way he described her. "Maybe I will see if she's interested in shadowing me one day. She'll be a senior in high school in the fall and she really should be considering her career choices. Whenever I've asked, she's merely shrugged and said she was still thinking about possibilities, but it couldn't hurt for me to give her an up-close look at one option.''

"There's always a need for young people to train for health care careers. Especially in nursing, I understand.''

Cecilia nodded. "In some areas of the country, nurses are in critically short supply. And there's a growing demand for midwives, with so many doctors shying away from obstetrics practices.''

"It will be good for her to see that work can be

challenging and enjoyable. From what I've always heard, the clinic is a pleasant place to work. Friendly co-workers, happy new parents, lots of cute babies.''

Cecilia lifted her eyebrows as she studied him across the table. ''Maybe *you* should shadow me at work one day. Have you ever actually spent any time in the birthing center?''

''Well…no, not much. My job has always been in other areas, so when I'm in town I'm usually in my office at Bingham Enterprises. Are you telling me it's not a happy place to work?''

''Obviously, I enjoy working there, but it isn't a theme park. In any medical setting, you'll find stress and tension and an occasional tragedy. Especially lately, we've—''

Realizing abruptly that she was being somewhat too candid with a man whose family controlled the workplace she was describing, she decided a bit more discretion was probably in order. ''All in all, it's a wonderful place to work. I wouldn't want to go anywhere else.''

His gaze was locked on her face. ''What did you start to say about the clinic before you suddenly remembered that I'm a Bingham?''

She sighed lightly. Was she really so transparent that anyone could read her thoughts or had Geoff gotten to know her a bit too well during the past few days? Six days, to be precise, she thought with a vague sense of wonder that a week ago she hadn't even known him.

''Cecilia?''

''I've told you it's been a particularly tense time lately,'' she reminded him. ''Everyone's nervous about the lawsuit—we can't help but think about how vulnerable we all are to such actions as we go about our work. It's a busy time, deliverywise, so we're all working pretty long hours. The drug crisis affects all of us in one way or another as we deal with addicted mothers and affected newborns. Detective Collins watching our every move doesn't help. One of our nurses is going through some sort of personal crisis, and she has been so jittery and tearful that it can't help but affect the people around her.''

''And the stress Mari's been under can't help but affect everyone, either. Tension always seems to work its way down from the top.''

''We all understand that Mari has a lot to deal with.''

''Maybe I should talk with her. See if there's anything I can do to help her out.''

''I wouldn't want her to think anyone in the clinic has been talking about her.''

''Give me some credit for discretion, will you? I'll simply say that I've noticed she seems stressed. Your name will never come up.''

''Thanks. I, um, guess your family's beginning to wonder where you've been for the past week?''

He shrugged and reached for his water glass. ''I doubt it. Everyone's busy, and I usually entertain myself when I'm in town.''

''So they don't know about…''

''Us?'' he inserted smoothly when she hesitated. ''I haven't said anything in particular, but Dad and Mari both know I was with you Sunday evening when you delivered that baby at the movie theater. Word of that sure got around.''

"Especially after the article appeared in the *Merlyn Mage*," she muttered.

"Well, don't worry. No one's making a big thing of our seeing each other. My family likes you. They aren't surprised I enjoy spending time with you. That's why I wanted you to join us last night at my grandmother's. We'd have had a pleasant dinner together, and you'd have spared me another evening of my grandmother trying to fix me up. This time she was pushing me to meet the granddaughter of one of her friends."

Cecilia found it difficult to smile in response to the ironic humor in his voice. She didn't find his grandmother's matchmaking efforts nearly as amusing as Geoff did. Maybe because she strongly suspected that Myrtle Bingham would never include Cecilia's name on her list of desirable brides for her beloved grandson.

Not that she wanted to be on the list, she assured herself. Hadn't she just asserted that she was perfectly content without a man in her life? That she was not like Brandy, so needy and insecure that she would sacrifice her own dignity to obtain the illusion of love? Though she longed for a child, she was content in every other way with her own company, her own accomplishments.

As for Geoff, he couldn't have made it more clear that he had no interest in settling down. In his own words, he saw a wife as someone else to answer to, someone else he would be obliged to keep satisfied and content.

He didn't seem to view a child in the same way, which reinforced Cecilia's suspicion that he thought of a child as a novelty. A form of slightly rebellious entertainment—like his motorcycle. Or an outlet for his creativity and self-expression—like his guitar.

She envisioned his role in their child's life as the noncustodial parent who made grand appearances with gifts and play dates and out-of-the-ordinary fun, while she would be the full-time nurturer, caregiver and disciplinarian. She could live with those roles. She knew plenty of people who had grown up under similar parental circumstances and had turned out just fine. If she didn't think Geoff would be a good part-time father, she would never have agreed to his terms in this partnership.

It would all work out, she promised herself. But in the meantime, she would just as soon not talk about his family's efforts to arrange a suitable marriage for him.

She promptly changed the subject, bringing up a local campaign to raise funds to spruce up some of the historic buildings in downtown Binghamton. The Merlyn County Public Library, for example, which was located in a renovated white clapboard house that provided five stories of books when the basement and attic were included in the tally. The library was always in need of upgrades and maintenance. The arts-and-crafts and bluegrass festival being discussed by community activists would became an annual event if successful and would be designated as a fund-raiser for the library and other local facilities.

"I think it's a great idea," Geoff said. "I've always said we need an annual festival of some sort to celebrate the area's history and unique character."

Relieved to have found a topic that interested him,

Cecilia kept the remainder of their dinnertime conversation centered on community affairs, rather than their own. All in all, she decided, it was a much safer topic.

Geoff insisted on helping Cecilia clean up the kitchen after they had eaten. The task took only twice as long with his help, she thought wryly. The way he kept distracting her with increasingly lengthy kisses, it would be a miracle if they got all the dishes into the dishwasher before he dragged her off to bed. Or maybe she would be the one doing the dragging, she thought after one particularly arousing close encounter.

He lifted his head from hers with a wicked grin. Only then did she realize that both his hands were beneath her knit top, his palms warm on her back. "I think the kitchen's clean enough, don't you?"

Mentally consigning the rest to a later time, Cecilia smiled. "Yes, I think it is."

Pulling her closer, he murmured, "Then maybe you and I could—"

His suggestion was cut short by the shrill ring of the telephone. Cecilia sighed deeply, tempted to let it ring. It probably wasn't an important call, she tried to convince herself. Maybe a telemarketer.

But when the phone rang again, she gave Geoff an apologetic look, extricated herself from his grasp and moved to the kitchen extension. "Hello?"

Her expression was even more apologetic when she hung up a very short time later. "Geoff, I'm sorry, but I—"

He nodded and cut in. "I heard enough to figure out that you've been called to work."

"Looks like I have a delivery to make. I saw this client earlier today, and I was pretty sure she would give birth at any time."

"A home delivery?"

"No. I'm one of the more traditional midwives on staff. My clients tend to prefer more standard deliveries with medical facilities close at hand—and so do I. Women who choose home deliveries or water births or other nontraditional methods are generally guided to other midwives."

"And yet you're still available for the occasional movie-theater delivery."

"We do what we have to do," she replied with a smile and a shrug.

"You need a lift to the clinic?"

"I'd better take my own car. This is a first baby, and she's in the early stages of labor. It could take several hours yet—perhaps all night. I can nap at the clinic if necessary."

Looking a bit disappointed but resigned, Geoff nodded. "Then I'll head on home."

She nodded reluctantly.

"Do you have plans for the weekend?"

"Not really. I have a birthing seminar to conduct tomorrow evening, which will last until around seven, but I'm not expected back at the clinic until Monday morning."

His smile returned with blinding intensity. "Just what I was hoping to hear. I'll pick you up at seven-thirty. Pack light—and don't eat dinner."

"Pack?" She blinked. "Where are we going?"

"Not far. You'll be less than an hour away from the clinic if you're needed. So what do you say? Want to sneak away for a weekend?"

A weekend with Geoff. Away from the clinic, the phone, the neighbors' problems. "I would like that. What do I bring?"

"Shorts, a bathing suit and a toothbrush. I've got everything else covered."

"A bathing suit?" Few women over thirty-five considered bathing suits their favorite type of leisure wear, and she was no exception.

His grin turned wicked. "Unless you prefer skinny-dipping."

"I'll bring a suit."

Putting on an exaggeratedly disappointed expression, he heaved a sigh. "Okay. Then I'll see you at seven-thirty tomorrow. I hope everything goes smoothly with your delivery tonight."

"Thank you."

She saw him out and then grabbed her purse and car keys. She was definitely going to have to make an effort to put Geoff and his mysterious plans for the weekend out of her mind for the next almost twenty-four hours, or she would never be able to concentrate on her work.

Chapter Eleven

Cecilia was having lunch in the atrium with Vanessa on Friday when her brother stopped by their table, looking so handsome and professional in his dark suit, white shirt and blue tie that she couldn't help beaming with pride.

He nodded to Vanessa, then spoke to Cecilia. "I thought I might find you here."

"Is there something you need, Eric?"

"Yeah. Hannah and I are going out to eat tonight. Someplace nice—Melinda's, maybe. We'd like you to come with us."

Cecilia moistened her lips. "Thanks, sweetie, but I can't tonight. I have other plans."

"Oh." He wasn't used to hearing that. After a moment he nodded and said, "Then how about if we do it tomorrow night, instead?"

Resisting an impulse to squirm in her seat, she said, "No, I can't tomorrow night, either. Actually, I'll be out of town for the weekend. You and Hannah go ahead and have your nice dinner. I'll call you as soon as I get back."

"Out of town?" Eric parroted blankly.

"For the weekend?" Vanessa murmured.

She lifted her chin. "Yes."

Eric planted his fists on his hips. "You didn't say anything to me about going out of town. Where are you going? Who are you going with?"

Cecilia glanced around, hoping they wouldn't be overheard. "I'm just taking a couple of days off. I'll have my cell phone with me, and I'll only be an hour away if anyone needs me."

"Surely you're not going away with—"

"Eric." She put a hand on his arm, squeezing to get his attention. "I'd rather not announce my personal business to anyone within hearing distance, if you don't mind."

He subsided to a disgruntled mumble that would carry no farther than their table. "You're going with Geoff Bingham?"

She should have known she couldn't pull this off in secret. "Yes. And I shouldn't have to remind you that I'm old enough to make my own decisions about my weekend plans without clearing them with you first."

"Doesn't mean I have to like it," Eric muttered.

"No, it doesn't," she agreed evenly.

Still frowning, he asked in the same quiet tone, "So where is this thing with you and Bingham headed, anyway? I mean, are we going to end up married to cousins?''

Vanessa propped her elbows on the table and rested her chin in her hands, apparently interested in that answer herself.

"No," Cecilia said firmly. "That is an extremely unlikely possibility. Geoff and I are friends, and we've both been working very hard lately. We need some time off for relaxation, and we've enjoyed spending that time together. That's pretty much the extent of it.''

She told herself it wasn't really a lie, since she had summed up the relationship quite well—except for the making-a-baby part she had chosen not to mention. If Eric was this freaked out by her going away for a weekend with Geoff, she couldn't imagine how he would react when she told him she was pregnant with Geoff's child. But she would face that hurdle when—if—it became necessary.

"Since I'm obviously not going to change your mind about this, I'll just tell you to have a good time.'' He leaned over to brush a kiss against her cheek. "Don't forget to call me when you get back, CeCe.''

"I won't forget. Enjoy your nice dinner with Hannah.''

She watched her brother walk away, still shaking his head in disapproval. And then she drew a deep breath and turned back to Vanessa. "Shut up.''

Vanessa lifted her eyebrows. "I haven't said anything.''

"You don't have to. That dopey grin says it all.''

"What happened to your policy of not dating men

who are prettier than you are? Not that I'm saying he is, of course.''

"Are you kidding? He's gorgeous."

"You're hardly plain yourself, kiddo."

"Thank you. But you're my friend and you're hardly objective."

"Perhaps. Anyway, I think it's really great that you're having a good time with—" she lowered her voice to a stage whisper "—you know who."

"You, um, don't think less of me for going away for a weekend with a man I've only known for a week?"

Vanessa seemed surprised by the hesitant question. "Come on, Cecilia. You're a mature woman. You've been married. It's not like Geoff's a total stranger you know nothing about. I'd say as long as you've both been clear from the beginning what you expect from each other so we don't have any broken hearts in the making, there's no reason at all why you shouldn't have a little fun."

Cecilia sat back in her chair, satisfied with her friend's blessing. For a moment she was tempted to tell Vanessa everything. But that was a bit more than she was prepared to share.

"Geoff and I have both made it perfectly clear what we want from each other," she said, instead. "No hearts are going to be broken."

"I'm glad to hear that."

Was that just a hint of warning in Vanessa's voice—a touch of concern despite her support?

Cecilia glanced at her watch. "I'd better get back to the madhouse. I've got an appointment in fifteen minutes."

"Me, too. And Cecilia?"

Gathering her things, Cecilia responded absently. "Mmm?"

"Have a great weekend, okay?"

She smiled. "Thanks, Van. I intend to."

It was an impulse that made Cecilia change into a bright red sundress when she got home from work. Maybe because she'd had on a red dress when she'd met Geoff last week, though this one was more casual. The spaghetti straps bared her arms and shoulders, while the ruffled vee bodice gave just a hint of cleavage. She wore hoop earrings for a gypsy touch and chose more comfortable sandals than she'd worn last week.

Maybe she was a bit overdressed, she mused as she pinned her hair into a loose roll, but she enjoyed dressing up occasionally after spending so much of her life in scrubs and casual clothes.

She decided it was worth the effort when Geoff saw her. After giving her a kiss that nearly melted her into the floor, he raised his head to ask huskily, "Have I mentioned that I like the way you look in red?"

"I think you just made that clear. You look awfully good yourself," she added, admiring the way his white shirt and well-tailored khakis showed off both his tan and his athletic physique.

He nodded toward the red wheeled bag sitting nearby. "Is this all you're taking?"

"Yes." She picked up her purse. "I'm ready."

A grin spread across his face. "You have no idea how glad I am to hear that."

It was a nice evening for a drive. Clear and not

quite as hot as it had been. Piano music played quietly from the CD player, proving a pleasant background without impeding their lively conversation. It was always a bit surprising to Cecilia how much they could find to talk about even when they'd only been apart for a few hours.

"Are you going to tell me now where we're going?" she asked when they had been on the road for just over half an hour.

"My family owns a vacation cottage on the far side of Ginman's Lake, close to the river. It's a place we go when we want to get away from the phone and the social calendars, yet we're still nearby if we're needed. I think you and I can have a nice, relaxing weekend there."

"It sounds very nice. How much farther?"

"Ten minutes. It's only a forty-minute drive from your house."

Which meant she could be at the clinic in half an hour if necessary, she figured.

She hoped it wouldn't be necessary.

The Bingham "cottage" was hardly a modest little vacation house, she observed when Geoff drove down the long gravel driveway. Constructed of rock and glass and sitting on a secluded lot that fell off to the lake in the back, the two-story house was bigger than her own home. Everything was so tidy and well maintained that she was quite sure they kept a groundskeeper on full-time retainer. "This is lovely."

"I haven't spent much time here since my mother died, but Dad comes fairly often for a fishing weekend."

Carrying their bags, he led her inside. She noted

immediately that the heavy wood and overstuffed up-holstered furnishings bore not a trace of dust. The main room was two stories high, surrounded by an upstairs balcony that probably led to bedrooms. The back wall was covered with closed draperies, but she would bet it was made of glass to showcase the lake view.

One wall was made up entirely of built-in book-cases to display books, family photos, electronic equipment, board games and knickknacks. A swing-ing wood door on another wall probably opened into the kitchen. The room was sweetly scented by the fresh flowers arranged in several scattered vases.

"Obviously you had someone prepare for our ar-rival," she commented.

"Mmm. Come with me and I'll show you the up-stairs."

Tagging obligingly behind him, she climbed the curving staircase and stepped into the first door on the left. It was a bedroom, of course, with a big iron bed in the center of the back wall and a dresser, ar-moire and nightstands made of distressed pine. The fabrics were in nubby golds and browns, and a thick rug was spread on the oak floor.

It was a warm, inviting room, and it wasn't hard for Cecilia to imagine snuggling with Geoff in that big bed. The image alone was enough to bring a light flush to her cheeks.

"Maybe you'd like to freshen up while I take care of a few last-minute details downstairs," he sug-gested. "I hope you're hungry."

"Are you kidding? I'm starving."

He smiled. "Give me fifteen minutes."

"I suppose I can wait that long—barely."

"I'll meet you at the bottom of the stairs."

She took advantage of the time to wash up in the big attached bathroom that was decorated in the same warm colors as the bedroom. She tidied her hair, unpacked a few toiletries and applied a fresh touch of lipstick. When fifteen minutes had passed, she made one last quick check in the mirror and left the room.

As promised, Geoff waited for her at the foot of the stairs. He smiled as he watched her walk down, his expression so appreciative that she couldn't help smiling in return. He held a white rose in his hand; he offered it to her when she reached the bottom step.

Touched by the gesture, she lifted the bloom to her nose to appreciate its scent. Only then did she notice that the draperies at the back of the room were open now, revealing a scene that made her breath catch in her throat.

Taking her hand, Geoff led her toward the glass wall. It was almost dark now, the sky a rich purple, the big, spreading trees casting long, deep shadows. The lake beyond the property, set into a deep valley surrounded by wooded Kentucky mountains, looked like a sheet of purplish-gray glass. A boat dock and fishing pier were accessible from the house by way of a long, sloping rock walkway with metal railings for safety.

But it was the stone patio just behind the house that held Cecilia's attention when she and Geoff stepped outside through a sliding glass door. Anchored by a big rock barbecue pit at one side, the patio was lined with inviting benches and big wooden planters that held Japanese maples, large lacy ferns and mounds of summer flowers. Multicolored paper lanterns glowed from wires strung overhead, illuminating a round wrought-iron table in the center of the patio.

The table had been set for two with china, crystal and silver. Silver-domed serving dishes, silver candlesticks and a floral centerpiece added elegance to the setting. Champagne chilled in a silver bucket. Soft music played from hidden speakers.

It was so blatantly, over-the-top romantic that Cecilia could feel her knees start to weaken. No one had ever done anything like this for her before. The only evening that had come close was the night Geoff had cooked for her at his condo—the night they had celebrated their decision to have a child together.

Bracing a hand on the back of a curvy wrought-iron chair, she looked at him through a sheen of tears. "You really have to stop doing things like this."

He trailed a fingertip down her bare arm. "Why?"

Because you'll make me fall for you. "Because you'll spoil me."

"I rather enjoy spoiling you."

"Still…."

Without waiting to hear further objections, Geoff moved to the table and lifted the champagne bottle from the ice bucket. Moments later he handed her a flute filled with the fizzing beverage.

"To our child," he said, touching his glass to Cecilia's. "May she be as smart and beautiful as her mother."

"Or may he be as handsome and charming as his father," she countered, then lifted the flute to her lips. She would only drink a few sips—just in case—but

this was most definitely a toast she wanted to ac-
knowledge.

He held her chair for her, then insisted on serving
her. The meal was perfection—a salmon-and-pasta
salad kept cool by ice in the bottom of the clever
serving dish, crisp asparagus spears, fruit salad. He'd
gone to a lot of trouble to have someone prepare all
this so that he'd needed only a few minutes to add
the finishing touches. That gesture alone illustrated
how completely different their lifestyles were.

She wondered if it would be confusing for a child
to have one parent with so much money and status
and the other parent who lived quietly and on a careful budget. A tiny part of her worried that the child
would be more impressed by Geoff's extravagant gestures than Cecilia's steady reliability. But she
wouldn't make this a competition, she vowed. Her
child would just have to learn that money wasn't the
most important thing in life.

It was fully dark now, and the lanterns glowed
against the starry sky. Tiny white lights were strung
in the potted trees on the patio. She would have to
do something like that on her much-tinier patio, she
thought. She liked the fairyland look.

"You've been quiet this evening," Geoff commented. "Tired?"

"A bit overwhelmed, I think."

"Which means?"

"I'm just not accustomed to such grand gestures.
The expensive dinners, the rocking chair…all of
this."

"Don't forget the herbal tea," he murmured.

"I'm serious, Geoff. Do you always do things like this?"

"What do you mean by always?"

She sighed, frustrated by his obtuseness and her own inarticulateness. "I mean, do you shower so much attention on all the women you…well—"

"Try to make babies with?" His voice was just a bit too measured now. "I can't answer that, since it's never happened before."

"Still, it isn't necessary to…well, to court me. I mean…"

"Cecilia." He didn't look or sound angry, but something in his tone let her know he found absolutely no humor in this particular topic. "I enjoy spending time with you. Yes, there's a purpose in our being together, but there's no reason we can't make the next few weeks special."

Now she felt terrible. Geoff had gone to so much trouble to make this a perfect evening, and here she was questioning his motives. Just because most of the men in her past had turned out to be all flash and no substance didn't mean she should judge Geoff by their standards.

But experience made a pretty darned good teacher, she thought as she tried to ignore the ripple of foreboding that went through her. She would be incredibly foolish to forget all the hard-earned lessons she had learned along the way.

Propped on one elbow, Geoff lay in the big iron bed watching Cecilia sleep. Moonlight streamed through the open bedroom window, bathing her in a soft light that suited her creamy skin. Her dark hair tumbled around her, and he remembered once wondering how it would look spread across his pillow. He was delighted that he'd had the chance to find out.

She must be tired, he thought, his gaze lingering for a moment on the purply smudges beneath her long eyelashes. She had talked about how busy they'd been at the clinic lately, and how much stress they'd been working under.

She had been up most of the night delivering the baby that had interrupted their last evening together. She'd told him the baby hadn't arrived until nearly two a.m. She needed a couple of days of rest and relaxation.

They'd had a very pleasant evening. After finishing their dinner, they had taken a leisurely stroll down the path to the water, where they'd sat for a while on the benches built into the sides of the fishing pier. Letting a companionable silence fall between them, they had listened to the water lapping against the pier and the bank.

Away from the lights of town, the stars had twinkled brilliantly above them, reflecting in scattered-diamond patterns on the surface of the lake. Hidden in the trees surrounding them, frogs and night birds had entertained them with an enthusiastic concert.

It had been a magical evening, as far as Geoff was concerned. He was so comfortable with Cecilia, so relaxed. Not only did she seem to have no particular expectations of him, she actually seemed uncomfortable when he went to extra trouble on her behalf.

He remembered her warning that he was in danger of spoiling her. Had it been so rare for her to be pampered? He knew she was close to her brother and that Eric took care of her home-maintenance needs, but she seemed to be almost entirely unaccustomed to nice gestures from anyone else.

Were all the men she had known—including her ex-husband—total idiots? Hadn't they realized that Cecilia was a very special woman, someone who gave so much to others that she well deserved to be indulged occasionally herself? If so, it was no wonder she'd been a bit wary of his motives.

She'd asked if he always made romantic gestures toward the women in his life. Truth was, he *had* done things like that for other women. He enjoyed planning nice evenings, got a kick out of watching a woman's eyes light up in surprise and pleasure.

But it had been a long time since he'd made the effort for anyone. And there was something different about the way he felt when he did something special for Cecilia. Maybe because she expected so little from him. Maybe because there was something different about Cecilia herself.

She was the first woman he had ever considered having a child with. Maybe because she was the first woman who'd ever asked him to, he thought with a smile. But also because she was the first woman he had ever seen as a suitable mother for his child. Darned near perfect, as a matter of fact.

He reached out to smooth a strand of hair away from her cheek. She murmured something in her sleep and nestled more deeply into the pillow. He wanted to lean over and kiss her, but he was afraid he would awaken her. She needed her rest. If he'd had to, he would have lain awake all night watching over her to make sure nothing interfered with her sleep.

This new level of protectiveness was different, too. Especially considering that he'd met few women more unmistakably capable of taking care of themselves.

He felt his smile turn slowly to a frown, and he wasn't sure exactly why. It seemed to have something to do with the strength of his feelings for Cecilia—feelings that were beginning to seem too intense considering the parameters of the relationship they had agreed to. While he'd thought it would be convenient to be good friends with his child's mother, this felt like more than friendship. Unnervingly more.

The odd feelings would pass, he assured himself. Neither he nor Cecilia wanted this situation to get all sticky and complicated. With the possible addition of a child, she liked her life just the way it was, and he felt the same way about his.

Just because she looked so absolutely right in his bed didn't mean he wanted her to become a permanent fixture there, he assured himself.

Funny. He usually made pronouncements like that with a bit more conviction.

Chapter Twelve

Cecilia must have needed time away from her usual routines even more than she had realized. Though Geoff's weekend place was less than an hour from her home, it felt much farther.

Rather than waking at sunrise and going nonstop all day as she usually did, she and Geoff slept late Saturday, then woke to a slow, delicious bout of lovemaking. They had a late breakfast, then walked down to the water to swim and sunbathe and be lazy until heat and precaution against too much sun sent them back inside.

She discovered something new about Geoff that afternoon. The man was a fanatic about games. Scrabble, Monopoly, Yahtzee, Parcheesi—he didn't seem to care which game she selected as long as they played. And as long as she made it a true challenge.

He loved to win—and he gloated unrepentantly when he did—but he was a good loser, accepting defeat with grace and humor.

She couldn't remember the last time she had played games like this, since Eric wasn't much of a player. Nor could she remember laughing so much in one afternoon—laughing until her sides ached and tears rolled down her cheeks in response to Geoff's foolishness.

They fired up the barbecue for dinner, threading chicken and vegetables onto skewers and roasting them slowly over the coals. They ate outside again, taking their time, talking about nothing more serious than the taste of the food and the merits of the music playing quietly on the unseen speakers.

Cecilia made a specific effort to keep things light, casual. The way it had been between them all day. She didn't bring up his romantic gestures—or allow herself to wonder how much of that was for her benefit and how much just from habit. She didn't talk about the clinic and the problems there. She didn't mention Geoff's impending business trips.

She didn't even discuss their hopes for a baby, since even that seemed like too serious a topic for this utterly relaxed day.

It was nicer this way. No past. No future. No plans or expectations. It was so delightfully different from her usual carefully planned and scheduled routine. And she intended to enjoy every single moment of it.

Geoff was the one who finally brought reality into the fantasy. They had gone back outside in the late afternoon when some of the heat had dissipated, and they were taking a stroll through the woods surrounding the house, watching birds and enjoying an occasional spectacular view from the hilltops. He turned to lean against the trunk of a tree as she enjoyed a particularly nice scene of the lake dotted with sailboats and fishing boats, with fluffy white clouds overhead and the blue mountains in the distant background.

"So when do you think we'll know?" he asked unexpectedly. "Whether we've hit a home run, I mean."

She took a couple of beats to shift mental gears. Keeping her gaze focused on that calming horizon, she said, "I assume you mean whether we've been successful in making a baby."

"Yeah. When should we know?"

"A couple of weeks, I suppose. Some of the new tests give results very early."

"So we could have an answer before I have to leave town?"

Now he had brought up two serious subjects practically in the same breath. She turned to face him. "Possibly. Of course, there's a very good chance that it will be negative. The odds against conceiving so quickly are fairly high."

He made a show of flexing his biceps. A light breeze ruffled his hair, making him look young and fit and so appealing her mouth went dry. "Don't forget who you're dealing with—Mr. Macho. When I'm faced with a challenge, I conquer it. I go about it the same way I play Monopoly. I play to win—no mercy, no acceptance of defeat."

Trust Geoff to compare making a baby to playing

a board game. And to make light of a topic that was so important to her that she wasn't even allowing herself to think about it this weekend.

She desperately wanted that test result to be positive. Of course she did. Once that goal had been achieved she could get back to her own life, and Geoff to his. No more juggling her work schedule and her evenings with him. No more awkward explanations about what they were doing together. No more grand romantic gestures. No more lazy days of swimming, laughing and eating beneath the stars.

And if she kept thinking along those lines, she was in danger of bursting into tears right here in front of Geoff.

"I suppose we'd better head back to the house so we can start dinner," she said.

He caught her arm when she would have started in that direction and pulled her against his chest. "I think dinner's going to be a little late this evening," he murmured against her mouth.

She wrapped her arms around his neck. "Is it now? And what if I'm hungry?"

"I certainly hope you're hungry," he said with a wicked grin. "I know I am."

Not even for a moment did she think he was talking about food. Raising her lips to his, she let herself enjoy the novelty of making out with a good-looking man on a shady mountain hillside.

She could go back to being sensible and practical Cecilia later, she promised herself. She would allow herself just one more night in fantasyland. And then it was back to the real world.

*   *   *

The real world was sometimes an incredibly hectic place. A week and a half after Cecilia and Geoff returned from the weekend house, she found herself in the middle of chaos at the clinic. Three women in labor at one time—somewhat unusual even in the middle of the Merlyn County baby boom. A full waiting room, including a few women who'd brought their unruly children with them. A woman who was probably going to be transferred through the connecting glass hallway to the hospital for a cesarean section, since her labor was not progressing well.

The entire staff was operating at a full run. Cecilia passed Mari, Vanessa, Milla, and Kyle during one full-out dash down the long hallway, and everyone looked as harried as she was beginning to feel. She didn't know what was going on between Milla and Kyle, but the tension between those two lately was becoming almost palpable. Whether it was smoldering attraction or growing antagonism, she couldn't say, but there was definitely something building.

Crystal Hendrix, the nurse whose personal problems were beginning to interfere noticeably with her work, looked more edgy than usual, her eyes shadowed, her hands unsteady. Cecilia couldn't help wondering if the planets were in some sort of weird misalignment or something.

Was *everyone* going through personal crises at the same time? Maybe that would explain her own totally atypical behavior of the past couple of weeks.

To make the situation even more tense, Detective Collins was back, lurking around like a gray-eyed predator watching for signs of weakness. He seemed determined to pester Mari with a few dozen new questions about the black market drug trade, but Mari simply didn't have time to deal with him.

Cecilia nearly collided with the detective herself as she rushed from an examining room to check on the status of a client who was in the transition stage of labor. Murmuring a barely civil apology, she sidestepped around him. She knew the man had an important job to do, but couldn't he understand that this was a terribly inconvenient time?

She thought longingly of her weekend vacation with Geoff, which now seemed so very far in the past. She'd been so busy since their return that her time with him had been all too brief. Even last weekend had been filled with professional meetings for both of them, two deliveries that had called her back to the clinic at inconvenient times, and other obligations that had seemed to have little purpose except to keep them apart.

She should get used to that, of course, since he would be leaving town before much longer, but she already found herself missing him. At least they had made the most of the time they'd had to spend together.

Forcing thoughts of Geoff to the back of her mind, she concentrated fiercely on the tasks at hand.

She was looking for Mari, for consultation about a new patient, when she overheard a snippet of heated conversation between the doctor and the detective. She had followed Mari to her small, cluttered office, where the door was always open to anyone who needed her. But Cecilia wasn't the only one who had been looking for Mari, apparently. Bryce Collins was already there.

Posed in a tense face-to-face confrontation, they didn't see Cecilia when she stepped into the doorway. She ducked quickly back into the hall just as Mari said, "Damn it, Bryce, can't you see how busy we are? I don't have time for this."

"Make time," he snapped back, his voice so hard that Cecilia instinctively flinched.

"How many times do I have to tell you that I know nothing about black-market drug suppliers?"

"Until you make me believe it. Something's going on in this clinic. Somebody here knows exactly where those drugs are coming from. And since you're in charge around here, *Dr.* Bingham, it's hard to accept that you're completely oblivious."

After what might have been a gasp, Mari said, "Surely you aren't suggesting I've been deliberately holding back information from the police."

"I'm not suggesting anything—I'm telling you that something is damned suspicious around here—and that a lot of the signs are pointing right at you. You have been pretty desperate to raise large amounts of cash for your new research facility, haven't you?"

This time it was Cecilia who gasped. She hadn't meant to eavesdrop, but she hadn't been able to avoid hearing that rapid-fire exchange. Surely Detective Collins wasn't flat-out accusing Mari of being involved in drug trafficking. Was the man completely off his rocker?

Even if Mari had broken his heart in the past, he had to know what an insane suggestion it was that Dr. Mari Bingham, to whom nothing was more important than this clinic and its patients, would have anything to do with something so evil and destructive.

Cecilia should probably make a hasty retreat, since this conversation was absolutely none of her business. But she really needed to consult with Mari, and she was beginning to believe Mari would appreciate the rescue. Besides, Cecilia was feeling a strong urge to rush to Mari's defense against this unfair attack, even though she knew Mari was fully capable of standing up for herself.

But a distraction came in the unlikely form of a young woman with wildly spiked blue hair and a pierced eyebrow. A new receptionist at the clinic, Heather was certainly an attention getter. Nodding to Cecilia, who had stepped somewhat abashedly back out of the way, embarrassed to be caught eavesdropping, Heather rushed to Mari's office door.

"Sorry to interrupt, Dr. Bingham, but we've got a situation developing out there in the waiting room. Some crazy woman is throwing a fit, saying she's hurtin' and she needs some Orcadol. She doesn't have an appointment or anything, but she said she got it here last time, and she needs it again. She's so strung out that none of us can make any sense of anything she says, so we think you'd better come."

Cecilia grimaced. She could just imagine what Bryce Collins would make of *that* jumbled summons, considering that he already thought Mari had something to do with illegally supplying the powerful and addictive painkiller.

She stepped into the doorway, determined to do what she could to deflect his attentions. "Mari, when you're free, I need to consult with you on a new patient. Late-stage pregnancy with a risk of preeclampsia."

Mari pushed a hand through her hair, then squeezed the back of her neck in a gesture that made her look even more like her brother than usual. "Thanks, Heather, I'll be right out. And, Cecilia, I promise I'll find you as soon as I'm available."

"Thank you." Cecilia turned to the officer then, her voice chilly when she asked, "Can I show you out, Detective Collins?"

He looked at her with narrowed eyes. "I know the way."

She nodded, then crossed her arms and waited, making it clear that she thought he was in the way of business. Heather also hovered nearby, looking curiously from Cecilia to Mari to the scowling detective.

Collins exhaled sharply, then pointed at Mari. "I'll be back. And if I find out that you're involved in this in any way, you can bet I'll do my job and haul you in."

Avoiding his eyes, she moved toward the doorway. "Just go away so I can do *my* job."

He stalked off, leaving the three women to glare after him.

"Mari, if there's anything I can do…" Cecilia began awkwardly.

Mari gave her a weary smile. "Thanks, Cecilia, but I can handle Bryce. Now, Heather, let's go take care of the crisis in the waiting room."

It looked like rain. Skimming down the highway on his motorcycle after escaping from a long, mind-numbingly boring day at the office, Geoff studied the dark clouds gathering over the mountains in the distance. He would bet that was a storm building on the horizon.

But in the meantime, he could enjoy the ride as he tried in vain to convince himself he wasn't counting the minutes until he could be with Cecilia again.

He wondered if he was coming down with something. Did the flu cause a person to walk around in an addled state or muddle his thoughts until he wasn't sure what was real anymore? How else could he explain his odd behavior of the past week and a half, ever since he had reluctantly brought Cecilia home from the cottage weekend?

He seemed to be waking with a new sense of expectancy each day. Rather than his usual rather grimly determined morning routines and obligations, he was singing in the shower, spending more time planning nice things to do for Cecilia than thinking about the business concerns that usually occupied nearly every waking minute of his days.

Odd, that, considering the limited nature of their partnership. Maybe it was because he was confident that the relationship was temporary that he could enjoy it so much, he rationalized. Maybe he saw his time with her as…well, as an emotional vacation of sorts. A chance to have a great time with a beautiful, sexy woman without worrying about where it would all lead.

Or maybe it was flu.

He slowed as he approached the city park. Although it was a weekday, there were still a few families taking advantage of the facilities on this steamy July afternoon.

One particular family caught his attention as he

cruised past. The man was tall with brown hair, the woman shorter with darker hair. She was a bit heavier than Cecilia, but the couple still looked oddly familiar. A small child bounced between them, an energetic boy of perhaps three.

Maybe he and Cecilia could bring their son to this park, he mused. They would laugh as he went down the slide and applaud when he navigated the monkey bars. And maybe that boy would have a little sister to play tag with and to—

Realizing where his thoughts were taking him, he shook his helmeted head. He and Cecilia weren't starting a family in the traditional sense. Their plan was to have a child together without sharing anything else in their lives. Cecilia had made it very clear that was all she wanted from him.

It was all he wanted, too. Right? The joy of a child without the drudgery of marriage?

And yet—drudgery seemed like such an inappropriate word when applied to Cecilia. She was so fascinating. So intriguing and challenging. And yet so restful. He thought it could very well take a lifetime to get to know every facet of her.

She fit with him in a way no woman had before her. He couldn't imagine anyone suiting him better. Not that he was looking for anyone better suited, he assured himself quickly. Everything was just fine for him the way it was.

He had his family, a successful career, and he could soon have a child to satisfy his natural desire to procreate. What more could he want. Right?

To be fair, the accident wasn't caused by his distraction with thoughts of Cecilia. Even with his mind so jumbled, he had followed every rule of the road, obeyed the speed limits, had come to a full stop at every intersection. Unfortunately, the driver of a rusty old sedan wasn't as careful. Either he didn't see the stop sign or didn't see the motorcycle, but he sped into the intersection at the same time as Geoff.

Geoff saw the car at the moment before impact. It gave him barely enough time to lay the bike down so that he didn't slam directly into the side of the big car.

As pain ripped through his left side, he only hoped his reaction hadn't been too little, too late.

The pace at the clinic was finally slowing a bit. Cecilia had already delivered healthy twin girls. The C-section was underway in the hospital. The hysterical Orcadol addict was on her way to rehab—though not without causing a major scene first. The waiting room was only half full now.

Maybe she would survive the day, after all, she thought as she pressed a hand to her aching back. It had been touch and go for a while there.

She still hadn't had a chance to talk to Mari. She checked on her next mother-to-be, who was, perhaps, a couple of hours away from delivery. Leaving her in the capable care of her husband and doula, Cecilia made another effort to have a quick conference with Mari. She still needed the consultation, of course, but she also wanted to see if Mari had recovered from the upsetting incident with Detective Collins.

She turned a corner into the hallway that led to Mari's office. As she walked that direction, she saw Mari step out, accompanied by a young man wearing an orderly's uniform. With her back partially turned to Cecilia, Mari pressed a stack of what looked very much like prescription slips into the young man's hand. He stuffed them unceremoniously into his pocket, turned and disappeared into the stairway at the other end of the hall from where Cecilia stood.

That had certainly looked odd, Cecilia thought, pausing in her steps for a moment as Mari moved back into her office.

And then she frowned and shook her head. She blamed Detective Collins for planting even the tiniest seed of doubt about Mari in her mind. There was no reason at all to find anything suspicious about that exchange, no matter how it might have looked to....

Hit suddenly by an eerie feeling of being watched, she glanced over her shoulder. Detective Collins lurked behind her at the very end of the hallway, arms crossed over his solid chest, one shoulder propped against the wall.

His gray eyes locked with hers, and his expression made her wonder if he suspected *everyone* at the clinic of being a drug pusher. Was he following her? Or watching Mari's office? She had no doubt he had seen the exchange between Mari and the orderly.

Probably because she was tired and grumpy, she took a step toward him with the intention of asking exactly what he thought was going on at the clinic. Before she had taken a second step, he turned and disappeared around the corner.

She was tempted to chase him down and ask her questions, anyway. Some remnant of common sense made her stop, take a deep breath and remind herself that belligerent confrontation was probably not the wisest way to deal with an overly suspicious officer of the law.

She turned back, instead, toward Mari's office. She would let her intuition tell her if Mari was acting in any way different than usual—though she still didn't believe there was even the tiniest bit of merit in Bryce Collins's accusations.

Mari was buried in paperwork. She looked up with a weary smile when she heard Cecilia in the doorway. "I haven't forgotten about you, Cecilia. It has just been an incredibly hectic day."

"For all of us," Cecilia agreed. "Our consultation can wait until tomorrow morning. I'll have some test results back by then. I'm quite concerned about this patient. She's determined to have a midwifery delivery, but I tend to think we should be considering an early cesarean section. I'd appreciate your opinion."

"I'll clear some time just before lunch, if that's convenient for you. We'll look over the file and the test results, and then we'll schedule a time when I can examine her for myself."

"Yes, that will be fine. Um, Mari—"

Before Cecilia could mention her strange encounter with Detective Collins in the hallway, the phone almost hidden beneath the papers on Mari's desk buzzed loudly.

Mari sighed deeply. "Hold on." She picked up the receiver. "Yes?"

A moment later she sat straight up in her chair, her expression shocked. "He did *what?* Is he all right? Okay, I'll be right there."

Slamming the phone back into the cradle, Mari jumped to her feet. "Cecilia, I'm sorry, but I have to go. Can you keep things running around here? I'm supposed to be in the conference room in ten minutes, but it looks like I'm going to be delayed.''

''Of course. I'll spread the word that you've been called away.''

''Thank you.'' Mari was already hurrying toward the doorway. ''I won't forget about our consultation tomorrow, but I really have to go now. My brother has been injured in a motorcycle accident.''

Cecilia felt her heart leap straight into her throat. Holding on to the doorway to steady herself, she lifted a hand to her suddenly tight throat. ''Is he going to be all right?'' she called after her rapidly departing supervisor.

Mari replied without looking back. ''Yes, I think so. I just need to go see him.''

Mari disappeared around the same corner Detective Collins had vanished around earlier. Cecilia was left standing in the hallway, her heart pounding so hard against her chest that she could hardly breathe.

She had no right to hurry after Mari to Geoff's side. He needed his family now, not his temporary…what? Fling? Lover? Neither term seemed to fit.

Putting both hands to her temples, she tried to collect herself. She had a baby to deliver. She had to put her emotions aside. And more importantly, she had to resist the impulse to abandon her responsibilities and rush to Geoff, even if it almost killed her.

Chapter Thirteen

Geoff climbed out of his car very carefully Thursday evening. The walk from the car to Cecilia's front door seemed a bit longer than usual as his aching muscles protested every step.

Confident that he looked fine, scrapes and bruises hidden for now beneath a blue shirt and khaki slacks, he held himself straight and rang the doorbell. Thanks to his helmet, there were no injuries to his head or face, but the truth was, he'd been damned lucky today.

Cecilia opened the door. Something in her expression made the smile he had donned for her benefit fade away.

"I, uh, guess you heard," he said when she only stood there, staring mutely up at him.

"I heard." She moved aside so he could enter.

He might have reached out to her then to give her his usual kiss of greeting, but her body language was perfectly clear: "Stay back."

She closed the door behind him, her movements very deliberate. "I take it you aren't seriously injured?"

He supposed there was concern in the question. She had spoken so mechanically that it was hard to tell. "A few scrapes. There was no reason for me to even go to the emergency room, but the cops insisted."

She nodded. Her arms were crossed in front of her now, and her dark eyes were so shuttered that he saw no expression in them at all. "I'm glad you're okay."

He raised his left hand to the back of his neck, then immediately regretted the habitual gesture. He lowered the arm very carefully back to his side, feeling his scraped elbow throb in rhythm with his heartbeats.

Perhaps she was angry with him for some reason. There was only one way to find out for sure. "What's wrong, Cecilia? Are you annoyed because I didn't call you? Because I knew you were busy, and my cell phone was smashed in the wreck, and I wasn't really hurt, anyway...."

Deciding he sounded like a babbling idiot, he shut up.

Cecilia seemed to rouse from her reverie then. Blinking a few times, she tucked a strand of hair behind her ear. "I worked late this evening, delivering a baby who decided during the latter stage of labor to take his sweet time coming out. I haven't been home long enough to start dinner. How about if we order pizza again? Or if you want to head on home and soak in a hot bath, I'll understand."

Because she sounded suspiciously hopeful when she made that suggestion, he asked, "Do you want me to leave?"

Her look of surprise in response to the blunt question was patently false. "No, of course not. I just thought you'd—"

"I don't need a hot bath," he said, deciding to pretend as though everything was completely normal until she relaxed enough to tell him what was going on. "Pizza sounds fine. In fact, I'll order. What kind do you want? Veggie?"

"Sure. Okay. Veggie."

She was definitely not acting like herself, he thought as he placed the order. Should he pressure her to tell him what was wrong or give her time to volunteer the explanation?

He decided the latter was probably the best plan. He never liked being nagged to talk when something was bugging him. So he really should give Cecilia some space.

But, being the impatient sort that he was, he barely made it back across the room before he asked, "So, did you have a bad day at work?"

"Not bad, particularly. Hectic."

"You must be tired." Could that be the explanation? Simple exhaustion. If so, he had just the remedy. A night of lazy pampering would do them both good.

"Yes, a bit."

He lowered himself gingerly onto the couch, then patted the cushion on his right side. "Then let's just kick back and relax and you can tell me all about it."

She made no move to sit down. "Actually, I think

I would like some coffee. Do you want something? Juice, maybe?''

He stifled a sigh, telling himself again to be patient and let her take her time. ''I'm okay for now. Thanks.''

She was gone for quite a while. She must be harvesting the coffee beans, he decided wryly. She was certainly brewing it so long it should be strong enough to walk back into the living room by itself.

She finally reappeared, carrying a steaming mug cradled between both hands. She seemed to be taking care not to meet his eyes. He waited until she had taken a seat—notably not beside him on the couch, but in one of the chairs. And her body language was no more open or encouraging now than it had been when he had first arrived. ''You're going to have to tell me what's wrong eventually, you know.''

''There's nothing wrong, Geoff. I told you, it's been a long day. There was a rush on our services. A strung-out drug addict made a scene in the waiting room. Detective Collins made an absolute pest of himself, even coming out and accusing Mari of knowing something about black-market drug trafficking. It was all I could do to keep from kicking him out of the clinic myself then, even though it certainly wasn't my place to do so.''

''It couldn't have helped your day when you heard I had stupidly wrecked my bike,'' he said, trying to imagine how he would have felt if something similar had happened to her. He didn't even want to think about that.

She scowled down into the coffee. ''No. That didn't help at all.''

Suddenly realizing exactly what she had said before he'd brought up the accident, he straightened sharply on the couch, muttered a curse when his whole left side throbbed in reaction, then said, "What was that about Bryce accusing Mari of drug trafficking?"

"I said he practically accused her. He didn't come right out and say those words, but he said he doesn't believe she's telling him everything she knows. He even implied that her ambition to raise money for the medical research center could make her receptive to drug money."

"I'll pound his face in," Geoff said between clenched teeth as a wave of fury rushed through him.

She answered a bit sarcastically, "Oh, that will help. You and Mari can request adjoining jail cells."

He made an effort to get his rarely seen temper under control. "I'll call our lawyer tomorrow and see what I can do about keeping Collins away from Mari."

"Maybe you had better ask Mari what she wants you to do first. She might not appreciate you rushing to her rescue without telling her. And she probably wouldn't be at all pleased that I've been reporting to you about what I accidentally overheard Detective Collins say to her in the privacy of her office."

"All right, I'll talk to her. I'll tell her I've heard he's been on her case and ask her how she wants me to handle it. I can't believe that guy would still be nursing such a grudge against her that he would let it interfere with his professional objectivity. There's no way he can honestly believe she would get involved in that kind of sleaze."

"Of course not. No one who knows Mari would believe such a thing."

"How did she take it? Tell me she slugged him."

Cecilia shook her head. "Of course she didn't slug him. She managed to contain her temper—and her dignity—very well."

"She should've slugged him," he muttered.

"I never realized you had such a violent side to you."

"Only when someone messes with someone I care about." And it occurred to him suddenly that he would be just as belligerent toward anyone who was making trouble for Cecilia.

Because he wasn't sure she would want to hear that right now, he said only, "Collins has really gone over the line. He couldn't have a scrap of evidence that Mari is involved in anything suspicious."

Cecilia started to say something, but stopped when the doorbell rang. Geoff wondered what it was she'd started to tell him. Something she knew about the investigation? Some reason, no matter how unlikely, why Collins may have set his sights on Mari. Making a mental note to ask her later, he watched as she set her coffee cup on the table beside her chair. "That will be the pizza. I'll get it."

He held up a hand to keep her in her seat while he rose, exerting all his strength to keep her from seeing how much the movement pained him. "I ordered. I'll get it."

She looked as though she was going to argue, but she must have known it would do no good. Settling back into her seat, she subsided into the same moody silence as before, to Geoff's exasperation.

* * *

Cecilia was struggling to act naturally with Geoff this evening, but she didn't try to delude herself that she was being successful at it. The truth was, she didn't quite know what she was feeling. Numbness seemed to be the closest description.

She looked down at the half-eaten slice of pizza on her plate, doubtful that she could swallow another bite. She wasn't usually the type to overreact so dramatically to a trying day, but this day had been more than ordinarily stressful.

"Tell me the truth, Cecilia. Are you angry with me?"

She couldn't meet his eyes when she answered. "No, of course I'm not angry."

It wasn't quite a lie, she assured herself. She wasn't angry with him...exactly. More perturbed with him for risking his life and scaring her so badly, which was so unreasonable of her that she didn't know how to explain it to him.

"Then what's wrong? Did something bad happen with one of your deliveries?"

"No. I've already told you how hectic my day was. Nothing specifically upsetting, just a series of complications."

And that, she thought, was the biggest lie she had told him yet. Of course there had been a specific incident that had upset her today. Hearing Mari say that Geoff had been involved in a motorcycle accident had shaken Cecilia all the way to the core.

She had managed to control her emotions while she'd completed her workday, even smiling and speaking cheerfully during the prolonged but uneventful delivery of the Claussen baby boy. And then, after tapping the hospital grapevine to discover that Geoff had already been released from the emergency room, she had come home and pretty much fallen apart.

Just remembering that period of secret anxiety between watching Mari rush away and hearing that Geoff's injuries had only been minor ones made Cecilia's chest start to ache again. Finding that she simply couldn't sit still any longer, she pushed her chair back abruptly and sprang to her feet. "I need some more lemonade. Can I get you anything while I'm up?"

She waited barely long enough for him to decline the offer before she rushed into the kitchen. Maybe if she had just another few minutes to collect herself…

Geoff didn't give her those minutes. He followed her into the kitchen, then stood blocking the door, his arms crossed, his expression grimly determined.

"I've tried to be patient," he said, his voice quiet but firm. "I thought you would eventually get around to telling me what's bothering you this evening. But it isn't working. You're not giving me any clues. What's going on, Cecilia?"

"I told you, I'm just—"

"Tired," he finished in unison with her. "But that doesn't cut it. It's more than that."

She reached for a paper towel and wiped at an imaginary spot on the countertop, just to give her unsteady hands something to do. "I don't—"

"Cecilia." He had moved to stand very close behind her. "If it isn't your work that's upsetting you, it must be me. And the only thing I've done today is get involved in a minor motorcycle accident."

Saying nothing, she crumpled the paper towel in her hand.

"Are you annoyed that I didn't call you? Or have someone else call you? I explained why I didn't. And besides, when I mentioned that someone should let you know what happened, Mari told me you were with her when the emergency room nurse called her— without my knowledge, I might add. Mari told me she had let you know it wasn't a serious accident."

"Yes, she said she thought you would be fine."

"So you weren't worried about me."

"Not worried?" Feeling something snap inside her, she threw the paper towel on the counter and whirled to face him. "Not worried? Are you joking?"

He looked surprised by her vehemence. "You mean, you were worried? Even though Mari told you—"

"Mari told me—as she left her office at a run— that her brother had been in a motorcycle accident and while she *thought* he would be okay, she was obviously frantic to find out for herself. That was the last I heard until a few hours later when I finally managed to find out that you had been treated and released."

Now he looked defensive. "I told you I thought you'd been kept informed."

"Right. You told me."

"Look, I didn't realize you would be so concerned. And while I appreciate that you were worried about me, I—"

She glared at him, wondering if he could really be so obtuse. "I just knew that motorcycle was an accident waiting to happen."

That made his eyes narrow. "Now you sound like my father and my sister. Both of them spent a couple of hours yelling at me this afternoon about the bike. Telling me how reckless and irresponsible it is for me to even own the thing, much less take it for an occasional ride."

She lifted her chin. "Maybe I agree with them."

He scowled. "Great."

Though she tried to hold them back, the words spilled from her, anyway. "Well, you do have responsibilities—to your family, who love you and depend on you—and to Bingham Enterprises, where you serve a very important role."

"And to you, of course," he added. "Were you afraid I'd broken my neck before I fulfilled my bargain to you?"

That made her jaw drop. "That is *not* what I was concerned about!"

He lifted his left hand to the back of his neck, grimaced, then dropped the arm to his side again. She had already noticed that he had been favoring his left side all evening. Heaven only knew what sort of scrapes and bruises he was hiding beneath his long-sleeved blue shirt.

When he spoke, his tone wasn't as cutting, but it was still aggrieved. "I really didn't expect *you* to lecture me about obligations and responsibilities. I thought you, at least, understood me better than that."

"I'm sorry," she said stiffly. "I realize I have no right to lecture you about anything."

Just as she'd had no right to expect to be called when he was injured, she added silently. No right to ask him to be careful. No right to know where he was when he wasn't with her. What he was doing. Or who he was with.

This was exactly what he'd made it clear that he didn't want from her—or any other woman. He had said he had too many people to answer to already. Too many expectations to live up to, too many commitments to fulfill.

He wasn't interested in a wife. Not even a long-term relationship. And she had thought that was fine with her. Exactly what she wanted, too.

Or so she had believed.

Because she understood now how unfair she was being to criticize him when she was the one who seemed to be changing the rules, she sighed and shook her head.

"I'm sorry," she said again—only this time she meant it. "I really *don't* have a right to lecture you. You just scared me, that's all. I was already stressed today, and when I heard you'd been in an accident, I guess I just freaked out a little."

She watched as his face softened a bit and his taut shoulders relaxed. "And I'm sorry I snapped at you. I should be grateful that you were concerned about me. And I should have realized you would be."

Still shaking her head, she took a step toward him. "Don't apologize. I'm the one who's been acting unreasonably. I suppose I do need to sit on the couch and relax for a little while, as you suggested earlier. Why don't I serve us both some ice cream—I have your favorite, chocolate—and then we can crash in front of the TV. Unless you need to go?"

"Ice cream and TV sound good to me," he assured

her and then gave her a decent imitation of his usual lazy grin. "But let's not use the word *crash,* okay?"

The sharp words they had both spoken weren't forgotten, Cecilia mused, but she and Geoff could put them aside for the rest of the evening. After all, there wouldn't be many more evenings to spend together before they returned to their separate lives.

He would probably be relieved to move on, especially after this. She didn't think it would be quite so easy for her.

Which was all the more reason for her to try to enjoy the remaining time they had together.

Sitting on the couch at Geoff's right side an hour later, Cecilia felt a bit of tension ease from her shoulders. They hadn't said much since they had moved into the living room, but the silence had been companionable. Having eaten their ice cream, they sipped the herbal tea Geoff had brought her and watched a new documentary on the history channel. The program was interesting, informative, quietly entertaining—just the sort of calming activity they both needed.

As the program neared its end, she noticed that Geoff was beginning to squirm a little—surreptitiously rubbing his left arm and shoulder, stretching his leg out as if it were cramping.

She set her empty teacup on a side table. "Are you in pain?"

"No, I'm fine."

She gave him a look that let him know he wasn't fooling her for a minute.

Geoff made a face. "Okay, I'm a little sore," he admitted. "Kind of stiffening up."

She twisted on the couch to face him more fully. "Just how badly were you hurt? Really?"

"Nothing serious. Really. As I said, it's just scrapes and bruises."

She reached out to unfasten the top button of his shirt. "So you won't mind if I check for myself?"

"Um—" He cleared his throat as another button popped out of its hole. "Just remember, it looks worse than it is."

"I'm a nurse. I know how to assess an injury." She slid the unbuttoned shirt carefully off his shoulders.

Had she not been a nurse, she might have gasped. Fortunately, her training helped her see with one long, searching glance that he had told the truth about the severity of his injuries.

Though the scrapes down his arm and his side were raw and angry looking and the bruises were already turning a rainbow of muddy colors, none of the wounds was serious. He was going to feel like hell for the next week or so—the soreness and stiffness would get worse before they got better—but he would suffer no long-lasting repercussions.

"You got lucky," she said.

He released a breath he must have been holding while she examined him. "I know. Dad blew a gasket when he saw me, but Mari convinced him I would be okay despite appearances. He's not a medical professional, of course, so it looked worse to him than it is."

"Were you given a prescription for pain medication? Because you might need something later."

"Mari tried to give me some pills to take, but I told her I didn't need them. I don't like to take prescription medications unless it is absolutely necessary. I can manage this with over-the-counter painkillers."

She frowned, both because it had been Mari, rather than the E.R. doctor, who had offered the pills, and because Geoff had turned them down. "I don't know, Geoff. You're going to be awfully sore. There's nothing wrong with taking something to make you feel better."

"You know what would *really* make me feel better?"

She looked up from his bruises to his face. His smile gave her a clue what he was going to say when she asked, "What?"

For a man whose left side looked as though it had been attacked by a cheese grater, he moved surprisingly quickly. He pulled her against his bare chest, letting his mouth hover only an inch above hers. "I'm prescribing my own medication."

She slid her hands up his chest, taking care where she touched. "And just what do you prescribe, doctor?"

"You."

She smiled against his lips. "I just happen to be available."

He might have murmured something about being glad to hear it, but since the words were lost in the depths of a spectacular kiss, she would never know for sure. Truth was, she didn't really care.

It was very…interesting making love to a man who had recently been injured, Cecilia discovered. When he had insisted that he was up to the activity even as she expressed her doubts, Cecilia had willingly cooperated.

On one condition, she had added. She would do all the work.

It was quite a challenge. She had to take great care to give him only pleasure and not cause him any pain. Oddly enough, doing so greatly enhanced her own pleasure.

She covered him with gentle, tender kisses. And then she covered him with herself. And when tears rolled down her cheeks as they experienced their release together, she knew it had much more to do with almost losing him that afternoon than with the physical gratification she had found with him now.

It was pain that drove Geoff from Cecilia's bed sometime around midnight. Gritting his teeth, he slipped stiffly from beneath the covers. He was relieved when she didn't stir. Remembering her description of her day, he knew she must be worn out.

He found nonprescription painkillers in her medicine cabinet. Though the dosage was two tablets, he swallowed four.

He really was hurting. He doubted that the four little brown pills would be nearly as effective against his pain as Cecilia's tender loving care had been earlier, but it didn't seem like a particularly good idea to wake her for another dose.

Wearing only a pair of boxer shorts over his sorely abused body, he prowled restlessly through Cecilia's house while he waited for the medicine to take effect. He ended up in the room they had painted together last week.

The nursery.

Looking at the maple rocker that was the only piece of furniture in the green-walled bedroom, he allowed himself a few minutes to savor the memories of that day that seemed oddly longer ago than it actually had been. The laughter. The kisses. The long, arousing shower that had followed their silly play with the paint.

And then his thoughts drifted forward. To the future that might be. He could almost see a crib against the far wall, and a tiny body sleeping peacefully in that crib. He could picture Cecilia lifting the baby from the crib and settling into the rocker for a middle-of-the-night nursing. And he saw himself, standing in the doorway to watch.

But no, that wasn't right, he thought with a shake of his head. He didn't belong in that particular scene. He wouldn't be here for feedings and baths and bedtime stories and first smiles. That was the agreement they had made. He would be the part-time parent, the one who popped in for weekend and holiday visitations, while Cecilia would handle the day-to-day responsibilities he had said he didn't want.

Hadn't this evening proved he was right about having someone else to answer to if he got seriously involved with a woman? After being chewed out by his family just for trying to have a little fun on his bike, he'd had to endure pretty much the same from Cecilia. Another lecture about his obligations to family and business. More wounded looks that had made him feel guilty for being in an accident that hadn't even been his fault.

So why did he find it sort of nice that she had been so frightened on his behalf?

"Geoff?" Cecilia's sleepy voice came from the hallway behind him. "Are you all right?"

Turning away from the empty wall where he had just imagined a crib to be, he responded. "Yes, I'm fine. Just a little sore."

He snapped off the nursery light as he went to meet her and to assure her again that he was okay—physically, at least. Emotionally—well, he seemed to be a little shaky in that area this evening.

Chapter Fourteen

Cecilia was on her way to Mari's office for the scheduled consultation Friday morning when she crossed paths with Vanessa. Because it was so unusual to see Vanessa frowning, Cecilia had to take a minute to stop and ask what was wrong.

"Everything is just so crazy around here lately," her friend complained. "Have you noticed it, too, or is it just me?"

"Trust me, it's not just you. I've been wondering if the planets are misaligned."

"Wouldn't surprise me at all."

"Is there anything in particular that's got you scowling now or just a series of events?"

Vanessa made a face. "I've been dealing with a mess in the medical supply room. Everything's rearranged. I couldn't even find the Orcadol. Someone put all the bottles in the wrong place."

Cecilia frowned and spoke quickly, "Orcadol is missing? Should we notify Detective Collins?"

Vanessa shook her head, making her enormous earrings swing wildly. She held both hands up in a calming and rather pleading gesture. "Lord, don't get the detective all worked up again. I didn't say anything was missing, just misplaced. The new security measures seem to be working well enough to satisfy even Detective Collins. The filing system, on the other hand, definitely needs some work."

It still concerned Cecilia that Orcadol had been incorrectly shelved, but she told herself Vanessa had the situation under control. She was just oversensitive about the subject, she supposed, after what she had overheard between Collins and Mari. "I'm on my way to a consultation with Mari. It shouldn't take too long. Want to grab lunch afterward and have a nice, long gripe session?"

"You bet I do. Find me when you're free."

Cecilia nodded and moved on toward Mari's office. Mari looked up from her usual mountain of paperwork with a smile. Obviously, judging from her expression, she was having a better day than yesterday.

"Thank God it's Friday," she said as Cecilia took a chair beside the desk in response to a wave from Mari's hand. "Those words have never seemed more appropriate than they do this week."

"I know what you mean. Vanessa and I were just saying something to that effect. It's been a madhouse around here."

"Speaking of which—I'm sorry I ran out of here like a crazy woman yesterday."

"I understood. You were worried about your

brother.'' Cecilia had pretty much been a crazy woman herself after that, though she had done her best to hide it.

Mari nodded gravely. "Yeah. I hate that motorcycle, and Geoff knows it. It's a miracle he didn't break his fool neck."

Were you afraid I'd broken my neck before I fulfilled my bargain to you? Cecilia could hear the echo of Geoff's resentful question in her mind, and it still irritated her.

"I'm glad he wasn't seriously injured" was all she said to his sister.

Mari's face softened. "Me, too. As annoyed as I get with him at times, I still love the guy."

Cecilia was becoming increasingly concerned that she did, too. And that possibility terrified her almost as badly as Geoff's motorcycle.

"Did you see him last night?" Mari asked casually. "He seemed anxious to let you know he wasn't seriously injured."

So maybe he *had* thought she'd been kept informed. It made Cecilia feel somewhat better that he had at least thought of her. She answered very casually. "Yes, he came by my place for dinner. He looked battered, but generally in good shape."

"Bet he's sore today." Mari sounded more amused than perturbed. Typical sibling, Cecilia thought with a slight smile. Mari had "I told him so" written all over her.

There was a bit more compassion in Cecilia's reply. "I'm sure he is."

"So you and Geoff have been seeing quite a bit of each other during the last few weeks, haven't you?"

Also typical big sister. Nosy.

"We're friends," Cecilia said with a light shrug. "He's been at loose ends while he waits for the next business jaunt, and it turns out we share a fondness for pizza and the history channel."

She had been making similar explanations so frequently during the past few weeks that it came naturally to her now. She hadn't even had to stop to think about how to respond without piquing his sister's interest.

Mari looked a bit disappointed by the prosaic response. "He does love the history channel. And he rarely finds anyone willing to watch it with him."

"Same here. Now, about this new patient I saw yesterday…"

Confident that she had adequately deflected Mari's curiosity—at least for now—Cecilia kept the conversation on business for the rest of the meeting.

She would leave it to Geoff to make explanations if a pregnancy test yielded positive results at the end of the month.

Geoff doubted that it was entirely coincidence that he ran into Eric Mendoza in the hallway of Bingham Enterprises Friday afternoon.

"I heard about your accident yesterday," Eric commented. "How are you feeling today?"

"Like I got hit by a Buick," Geoff answered wryly. "I've got some fresh-squeezed orange juice in my office. Want a glass? Or I could have someone bring you a cup of coffee."

The quickness with which Eric accepted reinforced Geoff's suspicion that he was in for a brotherly interrogation. "Orange juice sounds good, thanks. CeCe's the coffee fanatic in our family."

"CeCe?"

Eric shrugged as he followed Geoff into the spacious office. "I've called her that since I was a toddler. She raised me, you know. Our mother was always away at one job or another and Cecilia, who's eleven years older, was my substitute mom—except for the two years she was married when I was between eight and ten."

"She still seems to have very maternal feelings toward you." Geoff handed Eric a crystal goblet of ice-cold juice.

Eric accepted it with thanks, took a chair, then remarked as Geoff sank into his own chair, "You seem to be moving sort of stiffly today. Pretty sore, huh?"

"You can say that again." Geoff opened a drawer in his desk, pulled out a bottle of ibuprofen, shook a couple into his palm and washed them down with orange juice.

"So how's your bike?"

Geoff grimaced. "It's in ICU at the Harley shop. It's a mess, but fixable."

"So you're keeping it?"

"Of course I'm keeping it. I love that bike."

"Never had one, myself. CeCe would've had a nervous breakdown if I'd even suggested it."

"She does seem to have a rather marked aversion to motorcycles."

"I guess they remind her too much of her dad. Understandable, I suppose."

Geoff leaned back in his chair, studying the younger man's somber face. "What do you mean?"

Eric's dark eyebrows lifted, an expression that reminded Geoff forcibly of Cecilia. The Mendoza siblings were certainly a good-looking pair. "CeCe hasn't told you about her father?"

"No, she hasn't really mentioned him. I know he died when she was young."

"Yeah. He died in a freak whitewater accident. Capsized and broke his neck on a submerged boulder."

Geoff winced as he remembered his ill-tempered comment about Cecilia being afraid he had broken his neck before he fulfilled their bargain. "I, uh, didn't know that."

"Apparently, he was a real daredevil. Always doing something dangerous, keeping his wife and daughter worried about him. He raced motorcycles, nearly got himself killed on them a couple of times before the kayaking accident."

Damn it, why hadn't she told him? This information explained so much about the way she had reacted when she heard about Geoff's accident.

"She doesn't like to talk about her dad. Neither did our mother. I don't know a lot about Cecilia's father, but I know neither one of them ever fully recovered from his death."

Not only had Geoff unwittingly brought all those painful memories back, he'd even snarled at her when she had shown concern for him. He wished he had known all this sooner. He felt like a heel.

"So," Eric said after draining his glass, "when are you leaving town again?"

Was that a hint? "In a week or two. The arrangements are still sort of tentative."

Eric nodded. "I suppose you'll be glad to get back to a big city. You must be getting pretty bored with the limited entertainment Merlyn County has to offer."

"No, actually I haven't been at all bored."

"Mmm." Eric gave him a long, measuring look. "I haven't seen much of my sister lately. I understand she's been spending a lot of her spare time with you. Anything I should know about?"

Geoff tried to keep his expression unreadable. "No."

Not yet, anyway.

But he didn't blame Eric for asking. If some guy with unclear motives came sniffing around Mari, Geoff would want to know if there was anything to worry about. He was still considering finding Bryce Collins and making a few not-so-veiled threats.

He and Eric talked about business for a few minutes. Geoff asked about Hannah, and then Eric took his leave, obviously having more questions to ask but not sure how to phrase them. Geoff was left to pace his office, business completely forgotten as he considered the things Eric had told him about Cecilia.

Cecilia had only been back from lunch for an hour when she was summoned to a telephone. Patting the knee of a young woman who was in the early stages of labor, she promised to check back in soon. And then she found a quiet corner in which to take her call. "Hello?"

"Hello, CeCe."

The nickname was the one only her brother used,

but the deep, amused voice was Geoff's. "You've been talking to Eric."

"Yes. It was a very…illuminating conversation."

"That sounds rather unnerving."

"Don't worry. He didn't tell me anything that would embarrass you."

"That's a relief." Cecilia glanced at her watch. As much as she enjoyed talking with Geoff, she had a lot to do. "How are you feeling?"

"Fine. But I need a favor from you."

"A favor? What is it?"

"I need you to join me for dinner this evening."

She smiled. "That doesn't sound so—"

"At my grandmother's house."

Cecilia sank into the nearest chair. "Oh."

"It's sort of a command performance. My grandmother heard about the bike wreck, and she wants to see for herself that I'm okay."

"That's certainly understandable. But—"

"I need you there, Cecilia. Someone has to protect me."

"Why do you need protection from your grandmother?"

"She'll be much less likely to yell at me about the motorcycle if you're there. Not to mention that she could hardly try to fix me up with all her friends' granddaughters if I have a date."

"I don't know, Geoff. I'm really not very comfortable with the idea of having dinner with your grandmother. What's she going to think about us—being there together, I mean?"

"She'll think I've brought one of my nice friends

along to entertain her. She'll be delighted. My grandmother loves entertaining.''

"But I—"

"Did I mention that I'm pretty sore today? I'll hide
the bruises, of course, but my grandmother's sure to
notice how stiff I am unless there's something to distract her.''

The man was shameless.

When she didn't immediately respond, he sighed
lightly into the phone. "Don't worry, Cecilia, I won't
pressure you into going if you would rather not. It
isn't as if you owe me any favors.''

Completely shameless! Of course she owed him a
favor. A rather big one, at that.

"All right. I'll go.''

"Great.'' He seemed to have absolutely no remorse
about pretty much blackmailing her into accepting.
"I'll pick you up at seven.''

"Yeah,'' she grumbled as she hung up the phone.
"Great.''

Why, oh why, had she let him talk her into this?

Geoff arrived at Cecilia's house a bit earlier than
seven o'clock. As it was, he'd had to make himself
kill a little time before leaving his condo. His eagerness to be with Cecilia was a bit daunting, since it
seemed so uncharacteristic.

He could list plenty of things that were different
about this relationship from the casual and temporary
affairs he had enjoyed in the past. The way he
counted the minutes he was away from her. The way
he savored each one he spent with her. The way he
woke thinking of her every morning. Hell, the way

he found himself grinning at nothing in the middle of a busy afternoon.

He'd been accused of being a little slow when it came to relationship issues, but even he could figure out that there was more than simple friendship involved in his feelings for Cecilia.

Even his eagerness to have him join her at Myrtle's was a little suspect. He usually tried to keep his girlfriends away from his matchmaking grandma. While the excuses he had used with Cecilia about deflecting Myrtle's attention were all legitimate, they didn't fully explain his compulsion to invite her. Cecilia seemed to fit with his family. He and Myrtle would both enjoy having her there.

This was definitely getting complicated. Especially when he considered how reluctant he was to think about leaving town again in a couple of weeks. For the first time he would be leaving behind someone other than family whom he would greatly miss.

He wasn't expecting to spot Cecilia standing in the front yard next door to her house, involved in a visibly tense confrontation with Brandy and the notorious Marlin. Keeping his eye on that scene, he climbed slowly out of his car.

He couldn't hear the words, but he heard the voices—Marlin's arrogant and furious, as usual, Brandy's tearful and pleading, also as usual, and Cecilia's firm and authoritative. Geoff hesitated, unsure whether to get involved or stay right where he was for now.

The decision was made for him when the argument turned violent. Marlin must have said something about leaving, because Brandy launched herself at him, obviously trying to hold him there. He shoved her, making her fall backward on the grass. Cecilia immediately rushed forward, and Marlin whirled, one arm cocked back as though to strike her.

Brandy cried out, "Marlin, *no!*"

Forgetting his sore muscles, Geoff sprinted in that direction. If that thug laid a hand on Cecilia…

Some last-minute shred of common sense—or maybe a glimpse of Geoff charging toward him like an enraged bull—made Marlin drop his arm and turn toward his truck. Geoff caught up with him at the door of the ugly vehicle. "You must be Marlin."

A scowl darkening his rather greasy face, and a bully's cowardice reflected in his eyes as he faced the man who was older, taller and in peak condition— except for a few recent dings and dents, Geoff thought ruefully—Marlin responded wittily. "Yeah. So?"

"My name is Geoff Bingham." Pausing a beat to let the significance of the last name sink in, Geoff added, "I'm a friend of Cecilia's, and of Brandy's. And if I hear that you've laid a hand on either of them, I will make your life a living hell."

Marlin blanched a bit, but he tried not to lose his blustering defiance. "You can save your threats," he snarled, jerking open the driver's door of the truck. "'Cause I don't plan to see either of them ever again."

Brandy broke into wails as Marlin drove away. Geoff moved to assist Cecilia in helping the girl to her feet.

"I thought he was going to hit you," Brandy told Cecilia.

"I thought so, myself, for a moment," Cecilia said,

brushing a strand of red hair away from Brandy's tear-dampened face. "Of course, if he had, I'd have been forced to pound him into the ground."

Brandy hiccuped in surprise at Cecilia's unexpectedly fierce response. "You...you would?"

"Honey, I've told you before. No man—or overgrown brat of a boy—has a right to put his hands on you in anger. Ever. And I promise you, no guy is ever going to do so with me. Not twice, anyway."

"Why do you think he backed off?" Geoff tried to keep his tone as light as possible under the circumstances. "Bullies are all cowards under the surface. If they can tell someone's going to fight back, they swagger off."

"He said he wasn't ever coming back," Brandy said, sounding forlorn.

"Actually, he probably will—the next time he needs a cheering section. Or a punching bag," Geoff said bluntly. "You're the one who's going to have to be strong and send him away. Even if it means calling the cops to escort him off the property."

"He really can be sweet, if he could just learn to control his temper."

Geoff tried to hide the impatience that would serve no purpose at all in helping get through to her. "Brandy, you're an attractive, intelligent girl. You don't have to put up with being treated the way he treats you. You deserve better."

Brandy looked from Geoff to Cecilia again. "I thought I loved him. And maybe I still sort of do, but when I saw his face when he turned on you, well, he looked like a stranger. A scary one."

"You were seeing who he really is, Brandy,"

Cecilia told her firmly. "And I agree wholeheartedly with Geoff. You deserve better."

Brandy drew a deep, unsteady breath. "Yeah. Maybe."

"Remember the talk you and I had last week?" Cecilia asked, brushing a hand over the girl's hair again. "When I told you about that very nice counselor at the clinic? Her specialty is talking to girls and women who have been involved with abusive men. She can help you understand why Marlin thought he could treat you that way and help you see why you deserve so much better. You're hurting inside, sweetie, and she can help you. Will you let me make an appointment for you?"

"I don't know. I'd feel funny talking to some stranger."

"I know the counselor Cecilia's talking about, Brandy. She's very nice. *I* would talk to her in a New York minute if I had a problem I needed help solving."

Brandy looked at Geoff then, first with skepticism and then with slow consideration. "You would? Really?"

"Really." It occurred to him that she was accepting his input because he was a confident-sounding male. Because she still lacked the confidence to trust her own judgment. Perhaps counseling could give her the self-assurance she needed to prevent her from falling back under Marlin's control—or that of some other abusive man in the future.

"Why don't you go back in the house and wait for your grandparents to come home," Cecilia suggested. "Lock your doors, and if Marlin comes back, don't let him in. No matter what he says, Brandy. Because he *isn't* sorry and he doesn't love you. Not if he's so willing to hurt you.''

Shoulders slumped, Brandy twisted her hands in front of her. ''He won't be back tonight. He's too mad, and he wants me to be miserable without him for a night or two. It's what he always does.''

''Good. Instead of being miserable, you can enjoy your new freedom. Call Lizzie and go buy a new outfit without worrying about whether Marlin will like it. Smile again, Brandy. You're only seventeen. Enjoy it.''

''Let me walk you to your door.'' Geoff crooked his arm and gave Brandy a smile.

She looked at his arm, at his face and back at his arm again. And then, very tentatively, she laid her fingertips on his forearm.

He bade her good-night at the door, advised her again to talk to the counselor, then waited until he heard the door lock behind her before he turned back to Cecilia.

He had quite a few things to say to her, but not here. ''Are you ready to leave?''

''Yes.''

Only then did he notice that she was dressed for dinner in a sleek black-and-white summer pantsuit. ''You look very nice.''

She smoothed her hands down the front of her out-fit in a nervous gesture. ''Thank you.''

Belted into his car and on the road to his grand-mother's house, Geoff wondered how to start yelling at Cecilia without sounding like Marlin. ''You do realize that interfering in domestic-violence situations is extremely dangerous, don't you?''

"I heard Marlin screaming at Brandy again, and I just couldn't stay out of it. I went running over there without stopping to think about it.''

"And it almost got you punched by the little punk. You should have called the police.''

"He didn't punch me," she pointed out. "And if he had, he would have found himself in more trouble than he ever expected. As my brother would tell you, I'm not as delicate as I might appear. I was married for two years to a guy who thought being male gave him some sort of natural superiority. He kept pushing it a little further until I packed my bags and told him to go to hell.''

"I'm not questioning your spunk, Cecilia. You've proven enough times that you have plenty of that. But the fact is, you're a small woman, and he had four inches and a good thirty pounds advantage over you. He could have hurt you.''

The thought of Marlin's fist connecting with Cecilia's face made Geoff's hands white-knuckled around the steering wheel. "Damn it, Cecilia, you should have called the police. Putting yourself in that situation was—''

"Reckless?'' she murmured. "Irresponsible?''

He started to retort, then bit back the words. Okay, he got the allusion. He had asserted that she had no right to judge or criticize his actions; he had no more right to yell at her for her decisions. It was just that...

"You scared me," he admitted.

"Imagine that.''

He gave a deep sigh. "Okay. Point taken.''

Though she didn't respond, a sideways glance let him see her rather smug smile.

After another moment he spoke again. "Brandy's still got some major problems, you know. She's still liable to take Marlin back when he comes around again, playing the victim and telling her how nobody else understands him."

"I know," Cecilia said with a sigh. "I'm not expecting miracles. I just want to try to get her some help."

"I hope she appreciates it someday."

"If she could only figure out that she doesn't need a man to make her happy and fulfilled. I'm hoping that if she gets nothing else out of the therapy sessions, if I can talk her into going, she'll come away accepting that."

Geoff didn't know what it was about that speech he'd heard before from Cecilia that particularly bothered him this time. Okay, sure, he could accept that she didn't *need* a man. She had certainly proven that.

But that didn't mean she couldn't accept a man into her life as a partner, did it? An equal. Someone who valued her, respected her, acknowledged her strength and offered his own when hers wavered. Just as she would do for that fortunate man if she—

If she loved him.

It was the first time the word love had entered his thoughts in connection with Cecilia. At least consciously. And it shook him all the way down to his nervous-bachelor toes.

Chapter Fifteen

As nervous as Cecilia had been about the dinner with Geoff's grandmother, it was a surprisingly pleasant and stress-free evening. From the moment she stepped into Myrtle Bingham's marble-tiled foyer, she was welcomed like an old friend of the family.

Myrtle was eager to hear all the latest news from the clinic, and Cecilia tried to oblige during dinner in the quietly elegant dining room. She left out most of the problems they had been experiencing at the clinic lately, of course, but she had plenty of anecdotes that kept her hostess entertained.

Cecilia thought that she could certainly be excused for feeling as if she were dining with a legend. After all, Myrtle was the one who had founded both the midwifery clinic and, later, the school. The hospital and future research center had both evolved from her early vision of quality health care for this poverty-stricken area.

Myrtle had also been active in funneling some of the Bingham fortune into the public library, the popular public recreation center and other facilities that were so widely used by the residents of Merlyn County. Surprisingly enough, there were still people in the area who resented the Binghams. For their money, their influence, the old history of Gerard's business ruthlessness and Billy's ceaseless womanizing.

Myrtle, as she insisted on being called despite Cecilia's initial discomfort with the familiarity, was still active in the community. With the energy of a woman half her age, she worked tirelessly for her pet charities. She seemed to be almost girlishly excited about serving as the spokeswoman for the new hospital public relations campaign.

"Lilly makes things so much fun," she added, a trace of Boston still detectable in her voice after more than five decades spent in Kentucky. "Have you gotten to know her yet, Cecilia?"

"No, not really. I've, um, been rather busy since she was introduced at the reception." She deliberately avoided looking at Geoff as she spoke.

"So has my grandson, apparently," Myrtle said, giving him a look of fond reproach. "I've hardly had a chance to see him since he's been in town."

"Hey, you're the busy one," he reminded her.

"Yes, I try to stay involved in the community. While you, of course, are out crashing your motorbike and scaring your poor family half to death."

Cecilia stifled a smile at the elder woman's prim

rebuke. Geoff squirmed in his seat like a kindergar-
tener in trouble, then obviously regretted the movement. She suspected that he would have winced, but
he didn't want Myrtle to see him display any discomfort. It was only because Cecilia had gotten to know
him so well that she spotted the telltale twitch in his
cheek.

"It was only a minor accident," he protested.
"Dad probably exaggerated when he told you about
it. You know how he's been lately."

Geoff must have been delighted that his grandmother was immediately distracted. "What has gotten
into that son of mine lately, anyway? He's been so
cranky."

Cecilia almost giggled. *Cranky* seemed like such
an unlikely adjective to be applied to the distinguished and dignified man she knew as Ronald Bingham.

"He's made poor Lilly's job so difficult. He has
challenged every idea she has presented."

Geoff shrugged. "She seems to me like the type
who can hold her own against Dad—or anyone else."
Then he added with a smile, "Much like Cecilia."

"Then they're both women after my own heart,"
Myrtle said firmly.

Geoff and Cecilia shared a quick smile across the
table—one that Cecilia realized Myrtle had observed
with a smile of her own.

"Cecilia's not after anyone's heart, Grandma. She
claims they're much too high-maintenance organs."

"Oh, I really do like this young woman." Myrtle
beamed at both of them. "I hope my grandson will
bring you to have dinner with me again, Cecilia."

"Thank you. I would be delighted." But Cecilia wondered if the invitation would still be good if Myrtle knew what she and Geoff had been up to for the past three weeks.

Myrtle escorted them to the door after dinner. She repeated her warm invitation for Cecilia to join them again and then placed a hand on Geoff's arm to detain him for a moment after Cecilia stepped outside. "I like this one, Geoffrey."

He wrinkled his nose at her. "You like everyone who's single and female."

"That's not true. I didn't care for that brassy red-head you were seeing for a while."

"She wasn't brassy. I think the word busty is more, er, amply descriptive of her."

Myrtle lightly slapped his hand. "You are so bad. Now go out there and charm that pretty young lady before she comes to her senses about you and takes to her heels."

"I'm so touched by your confidence in me." He leaned over to kiss her soft cheek on his way out the door.

As he climbed into his car, he thought about his grandmother's words. "That pretty young woman." Granted, Cecilia *was* a pretty young woman, but not quite as young as the women Myrtle had been practically throwing at him for the past few years. Because Cecilia looked younger than she was, Myrtle might not be aware that Cecilia was actually five years older than he.

Not that Myrtle was hung up about such things. It was just that she was so obsessed with seeing a new generation of Binghams in Merlyn County. Of course, she didn't realize that Geoff was already working on that part.

"I like your grandmother."

Rousing himself from his reverie, Geoff smiled at Cecilia. "So do I."

"She's so energetic. So clever and funny. So…so inspirational."

"She likes you, too."

"You have a nice family, Geoff. Our baby will be very lucky to be a Bingham. I just hope…"

"What do you hope?"

"I hope your family won't think less of me—or the baby—because we're going about this…well, the way we are."

His first instinct was to instantly and heatedly deny any such thing. But something held him back. Surely it couldn't be fear that she was right?

His family wasn't like that. Hell, *all* his paternal cousins had been born out of wedlock. His child would be…just another illegitimate Bingham.

He drove into Cecilia's driveway, parked in front of her door, then sat staring blindly out the windshield until she cleared her throat to get his attention. "Aren't we going in?"

"Going in?"

She snapped her fingers. "Earth to Geoff. Are you in there? This is where I live."

"Oh, yeah, right." He looked at her front door and suddenly shook his head. "Listen, Cecilia, would you mind if I don't come in tonight? I hate to admit this, but I'm so sore I can hardly move. I think I'll go home and soak in the whirlpool for a while."

"No, of course I don't mind." She sounded more concerned than disappointed. "Are you sure you'll be okay? Is there anything I can do for you?"

Feeling just a bit guilty for the prevarication—though God knew he was pretty darned sore—he shook his head. "I can handle it. I'll call you tomorrow, okay?"

"All right. If you're sure you'll be okay."

"Positive." He reached for his door handle. "Let me walk you to your door."

"Don't be ridiculous." She laid a hand on his arm to hold him in his seat. "I'm perfectly capable of walking myself inside. You just go take care of those aches and pains."

He ignored the aches and pains long enough to lean over and give her a slow, thorough kiss. "Good night, Cecilia."

Her soft smile let him know how much she had enjoyed the embrace. "Good night, Geoff. I hope you feel better tomorrow."

So did he, he thought as she closed the car door behind her. Because he was feeling pretty lousy right now—and it had very little to do with the motorcycle accident.

He watched her walk to her door, her steps so brisk and confident. So clearly not in need of anyone's escort.

He really needed some time alone to think. Because he seemed to have gotten himself into a situation here that was more potentially life changing than he could ever have imagined.

Although Geoff called Cecilia on Saturday, as he had promised, he didn't come by to see her at all. He was snowed under, he explained, playing golf with his father and some potential investors, followed by a business dinner, followed by a consultation with his father and some of the other Bingham Enterprises executives about the upcoming, though still tenuous, fund-raising trip to Boston.

She had plenty to do to keep her busy while Geoff was otherwise occupied. Housework, shopping, that sort of thing. One thing she wouldn't think about today was that trip to Boston he had mentioned, she promised herself. While she knew Geoff's time here was limited, and that once he left for the next extended business trip their affair would most likely be over, she didn't want to dwell on that just yet.

He had sounded busy, she thought, glancing at the phone. A bit harried. But there had been something more in his voice. Something that sent her intuition into overdrive.

He'd been acting rather oddly ever since they had left his grandmother's house last night, she reflected, wandering aimlessly around her house in search of chores with which to distract herself from his absence. Replaying that lovely dinner in her mind, she couldn't imagine what might be bothering Geoff about it.

Unless seeing her there had made him realize exactly how different they were, after all? Wasn't that something she had been too keenly aware of since the beginning? Geoff had always acted as though the differences in their ages, incomes and social backgrounds didn't bother him, but maybe he'd just never pictured her at his grandmother's table before.

Or maybe she was being paranoid, she told herself

with a scowl, and maybe he was still hurting from his close contact with the pavement.

Still…

It wasn't as if she had ever implied to Geoff that she wanted to be a part of his family. Just the opposite, in fact. She'd turned down several invitations to join them for various occasions, accepting yesterday's dinner invitation only because he had given her little other choice.

She had promised him that she wasn't angling for marriage or commitment. Just a baby. And while her feelings about those things might have undergone a few changes during the past weeks—as well as her feelings for Geoff—she was still resigned to the reality of raising their child alone. As contentedly alone as she could manage, anyway.

She just wished she knew what was worrying him so she could reassure him. Once she managed to reassure herself, of course.

Geoff was called out of town on Sunday. He explained to Cecilia in a quick telephone call that he would only be gone for a couple of days this time, that it was a business fund-raising opportunity he simply couldn't let pass. Something about a science foundation grant for research that had just become available—he'd been rather sketchy in his explanation.

As disappointed as she was that he'd had to leave, and as bewildered as she was by the fact that the trip had come up on such short notice, she told herself she should use this time to get used to his absence. She had a busy schedule of her own. To be honest, having him underfoot would have been inconvenient.

Nice speech, she told herself as she stared glumly into the mirror on Tuesday morning before work. Too bad she didn't believe it.

She was fully capable of living without Geoff in her life. She was even capable of being happy again on her own, as she'd been for the most part before that reception at the clinic. But she missed him. Much more than she had ever expected.

He called her that evening from Maryland, and this time she had no doubt that something had changed in his behavior toward her. For the first time ever, their conversation was stilted, their silences awkward.

She wasn't sure if Geoff simply wanted to end the relationship now or if he was sorry he'd ever gotten himself into it, but from the way he was acting toward her, it wouldn't have surprised her either way. She only hoped she could be composed and dignified when he finally got up the nerve to break it to her.

Sitting in one of the spring chairs on her tiny patio late Tuesday afternoon, she thought back over their time together. She could almost see him standing at her gate on that first Saturday, when he had agreed to help her with her rather quirky plan to have a baby. And she would never forget those summer nights on the much-bigger patio at his weekend house, the leisurely dinners eaten under the stars and paper lanterns. Painting her nursery. Holding hands at the movie theater. Delivering a baby together. Maybe making one together.

That was the one thing that bothered her most— other than how much she was going to miss him, of course. She still didn't know if their lovemaking had led to anything more than memories that would last for the rest of her lifetime. Maybe it was rushing it a bit, but she thought she would try one of the early detection tests tomorrow after work.

She glanced toward the empty backyard next door. Brandy wasn't there this week. Her grandparents had taken her away for a brief vacation before they started the family therapy sessions Cecilia had set up for them. They had a tough time ahead of them yet, but she wanted to believe they would work things out. And that Brandy would find a path that would lead to happiness and fulfillment, not the misery she had been headed for with Marlin.

Marlin hadn't been back. Maybe Geoff had scared him, or maybe he'd just moved on to the next vulnerable victim, but, at least for now, he was staying away from Brandy. Cecilia hoped the girl's next boyfriend would be worthy of her affection. Someone kind and respectful and caring and strong.

Someone like Geoff.

Feeling uncomfortably like a lovesick teenager herself, Cecilia groaned and hid her face in her hands. She would get through this, she promised herself. As soon as she knew for certain whether she was pregnant—and admittedly, the odds were against that—she could concentrate fully on her work again. Her nice home. Her beloved brother and soon-to-be sister-in-law. Hannah's baby, whom they would soon welcome into the family. She would enjoy being an aunt.

Telling herself she had all anyone could ask for, she pushed herself out of the spring chair and headed back inside, trying to convince herself that it was the sunset making her view hazy and not the sheen of tears in her eyes.

*   *   *

Cecilia walked straight to her bedroom upon arriving home from work Wednesday evening, leaving the package she'd picked up on the way home sitting on the coffee table. Before she faced the stress of taking that test, she wanted to get as comfortable as possible.

She changed from her work clothes into a bright-blue T-shirt and a pair of soft cotton blue-plaid dorm pants. Pushing her bare feet into a pair of white terry slippers, she tied her hair into a loose ponytail.

It wasn't quite 7:00 p.m. yet, but she didn't plan to go out again this evening, nor was she expecting company. Geoff hadn't called today. If he was trying to pull away from her gradually, he was doing a fine job of it. She was coming to terms with the end of their affair, but that didn't mean it wasn't painful.

Maybe she would make herself something to eat before she took the test. A salad, perhaps. Or a bowl of soup.

She was stalling. The truth was, she was still so nervous about taking the test that she needed a bit more time to work up the courage.

It was early. The results might not be reliable, especially if it came back negative. A false negative was more likely than a false positive. But for some irrational reason, she thought she would know whether the results she received were true.

She wondered if she should wait until Geoff was here. Perhaps he would feel that he deserved to find out at the same time she did. But then, he was the one who had abruptly pulled away. She didn't even have a telephone number for him. And she couldn't wait any longer.

She had the test in her hands and had just turned toward the bathroom when the doorbell rang. After a moment of paralysis, she stuffed the box beneath a cushion on the couch and moved toward the door. There were only two people she could think of who might be on the other side. Her brother. Or Geoff.

She opened the door. "Geoff."

His expression was hard to read. There seemed to be a sense of…resolve about him that she didn't quite understand. Was he here to tell her once and for all that it was over between them? "Come in."

"You look very comfortable," he said as he closed the door behind him.

"I wasn't expecting company."

"I should have called you. I've only been in town for a short while. I came here straight from the airport."

"Then you must be hungry. Would you like me to make you a sandwich? A bowl of soup? I haven't eaten myself, actually." She sounded nervous, she thought. Even to her own ears, her voice seemed an octave higher than normal.

"Anything sounds good. While we eat, we can talk. I have a few things I want to discuss with you."

Which was almost as frightening a prospect as taking the pregnancy test, she mused. "Have a seat. I'll see what I have on hand for dinner. And then we can talk."

She wasn't gone long. When she returned after only a couple of minutes to ask him whether he preferred chicken noodle or tomato soup, she found him sitting on the couch with the pregnancy test in his hands.

He looked up when she came to an abrupt stop just

inside the doorway. "You choose odd places to store these things."

She twisted her fingers in front of her. "I, um, was holding it when the doorbell rang. Since I didn't know who it was…"

The rest seemed self-explanatory.

"Were you going to take this test tonight?"

She nodded. "I couldn't wait any longer."

His expression was even harder to read now than it had been before. "I see."

"It's probably going to be negative, of course. It's highly unlikely that I conceived so quickly. I'm prepared for that, but I would like to know for certain."

He nodded. "So how long does it take to get an answer?"

"Just a few minutes."

"Oh."

Now they were both staring at the box. Cecilia abruptly held out her hand. "Let's get this over with. I'll be right back."

"You're going to take it now?"

She answered on a sudden surge of confidence, "Yes. It's probably best if we know the results before we have that talk you came here for, don't you think?"

Geoff hesitated, and then he nodded. "Maybe it would be better to know the results before we talk."

With her heart in her throat, Cecilia turned toward the bedroom.

Ten minutes later they stood outside her bathroom door, staring at each other as the minutes counted down.

"Nerve-racking, isn't it?" Geoff asked, his mouth tilting into a weak semblance of his usual smile.

"You could say that again."

"I know you're hoping for a positive sign."

She would have thought she would be praying for a positive. But suddenly she wondered if that was really what she wanted, after all. Looking surreptitiously through her lashes at Geoff, she wondered if saying hello to a child would mean saying goodbye to the love of her life.

Not that Geoff would be thrilled to hear himself described that way, of course.

"Why, yes," she said, attempting a smile of her own. "Aren't you?"

"I'm not sure."

She felt her eyes widen. Was he choosing this moment to tell her he'd changed his mind about having a child with her? If so, he had really lousy timing. "Um—"

"Do you want to know why I'm not sure?"

She swallowed. "Yes." *Maybe.*

He leaned against the hallway wall, his arms crossed over his chest. And now she thought she could finally read something in his expression. It looked a lot like the nervousness she felt. "I've done a lot of thinking about us during the past five days. About what we've been trying to do."

"And?"

"And…I realized that I've changed my mind. Only I'm afraid it's too late now to change the terms of our agreement."

"You've changed your mind," she repeated flatly. "Well, that's fine. If the test is positive, we can just go back to the agreement I originally suggested. I'll raise the baby alone, and you can go back to the life you had before.''

He shook his head impatiently. ''That's the problem. I don't *want* to go back to the life I had before.''

He moved suddenly, his hands gripping her forearms in a firm hold that was still somehow gentle. ''You know how I told you that I always thought of marriage as a cage? That a wife would be just another responsibility I didn't want to deal with?''

''I—'' She had to clear her throat as a wave of jumbled emotions swept through her. ''I remember.''

''During the past few days it has occurred to me that maybe I've been looking at it all wrong. Maybe it's possible for a wife to be a partner. A friend. A lifelong lover. Someone to share my burdens, not add to them. And someone for whom I could do the same.''

Her heart was pounding so hard in her throat that she had trouble speaking. ''That's…one way of looking at it, I guess.''

His voice was suddenly husky. ''What if I tell you that I don't want the test to be positive if it means saying goodbye to what we've found together over the past three weeks?''

She moistened her lips with the tip of her tongue, reading the sincerity in his eyes. ''What if I were to say I feel the same way?''

His fingers tightened on her shoulders just enough to pull her a bit closer to him. ''What if I tell you that I want to marry you—whatever the results of that test?''

She placed her hands on his chest, exerting just

enough pressure to hold them apart. "That would depend on why you're asking. Because if it's only for the child's sake or out of some overdeveloped sense of Bingham responsibility or if you've decided that you should make your grandmother happy and get married—"

"What if I tell you it's because I love you with all my heart and soul, and I want to make a real family with you?"

After a brief, taut pause, she whispered, "That might make a difference."

He lifted one hand to cup her flushed cheek. "I've been aware for some time that there was something missing in my life. A hole I tried to fill with business successes and occasional minor rebellions—like the motorcycle. And then I saw you at that reception. I know now that leaving you would tear a hole in my life that no amount of work or financial success would fill."

"Are you sure, Geoff? Because we haven't really known each other very long. And you were so positive that you didn't want this."

"I was an idiot. And a coward. And it doesn't matter how long we've known each other. We've hardly done anything the usual way so far, have we?"

She couldn't help but smile at that. "No. I suppose we haven't."

"You haven't answered me, Cecilia. Will you marry me?"

Nerves gripped her again. "We're so different."

"Don't start with the age thing again," he groaned. "How many times do I have to tell you that doesn't matter to me?"

"It might matter to your grandmother and your father if it turns out that I can't produce another little Bingham," she muttered.

"I don't care. We'll adopt. We'll get a puppy. Just say we'll be together."

Her eyebrows rose. "A puppy?"

His mouth hovered just above hers. "Whatever you want. I love you, Cecilia Mendoza. Tell me you'll marry me."

She waited until he had released her from a tender, knee-melting kiss before speaking again, "I won't be a submissive wife. I tend to be the independent type."

He kissed her again before replying. "You'll have to be. I'll still have to travel a lot, at least for the next couple of years. Since I doubt that you'll want to leave your job, we'll probably have to spend some time apart, but we'll make the most of our time together."

This time she was the one who pressed a quick kiss to his lips. "I can handle that."

He drew back, his eyes searching her face. "Is that a yes?"

"It's a yes—if you're absolutely sure. I love you, Geoff. I think I fell in love with you when you smiled at me and offered me a bite of your strawberry at the reception."

This kiss lasted so long that they were both gasping when it ended.

"I can't believe we're engaged," Cecilia said when she could speak again. "Eric is going to faint."

"Think he'll approve?"

"I'm sure he will. What about your father and Mari?"

"They'll be delighted that someone is willing to take me in hand. And since my grandmother already loves you, we shouldn't have any trouble with family."

"Oh, heavens. Speaking of family." Cecilia looked anxiously toward the bathroom doorway.

Geoff took her hand. "Let's look together, shall we? And Cecilia—if it's negative, I'm willing to keep trying to make a baby until we both collapse from exhaustion."

His exaggeratedly noble tone made her laugh, albeit a bit nervously. They crossed the room slowly, and she suspected that Geoff was as nervous as she was when she drew the plastic stick from its holder.

"Well?" he asked, when she took a moment to get her emotions under control.

The look she gave him must have said it all.

"It's positive?"

She nodded. The planets were definitely out of alignment, she thought in a daze, but this time she wasn't complaining.

Looking disgustingly proud of himself, Geoff grinned and swept her into his arms. "Maybe we should keep working at it, anyway—just to make sure."

Her head spinning with the realization that she had just been given everything she had ever wanted—and so much more—she wrapped her arms around his neck. "I love the way you think."

"And I will love you," he murmured, tumbling her onto the bed, "for the rest of my life."

"I'll expect that in writing," she warned.

''A woman after my own heart,'' he whispered as his hands and his lips began to roam.

This time, she didn't bother to argue with him.

* * * * *

Don't miss the continuation of
MERLYN COUNTY MIDWIVES
Delivering the miracle of life...and love!

BLUEGRASS BABY
by Judy Duarte
Silhouette Special Edition 1598
Available March 2004

FOREVER...AGAIN
by Maureen Child
Silhouette Special Edition 1604
Available April 2004

IN THE ENEMY'S ARMS
by Pamela Toth
Silhouette Special Edition 1610
Available May 2004

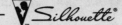

If you enjoyed what you just read,
then we've got an offer you can't resist!

Take 2 bestselling love stories FREE!

Plus get a FREE surprise gift!

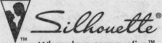

A special collector's volume featuring
Nora's sexiest bachelor brothers ever!

#1 *New York Times* bestselling author

NORA ROBERTS

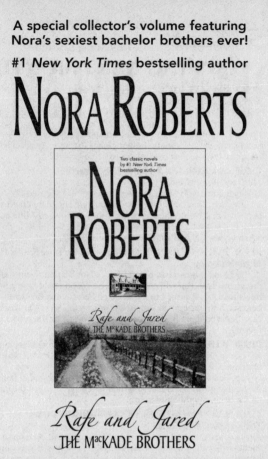

Rafe and Jared
THE MᶜKADE BROTHERS

These brothers are looking for trouble—and always
finding it. Now they're on a collision course with love!

Watch for Shane's and Devin's stories, coming in June 2004!

Silhouette®
Where love comes alive™

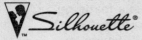

COMING NEXT MONTH

#1597 ISN'T IT RICH?—Sherryl Woods
Million Dollar Destinies

Single and happy-that-way Richard Carlton refused to act on the foolish feelings that PR consultant Melanie Hart inspired. Melanie brought passion to his too-organized, too-*empty* life. But soon her bundles of energy were no longer giving Richard a headache as much as a whole new outlook on life…and love!

#1598 BLUEGRASS BABY—Judy Duarte
Merlyn County Midwives

Dedicated midwife Milla Johnson was unfairly accused of malpractice…and only bad-boy doctor Kyle Bingham could save her. But what would the jury think if they discovered Milla and Kyle had shared a night of passion? And what would Kyle do when he learned Milla now carried their child?

#1599 TAKE A CHANCE ON ME—Karen Rose Smith
Logan's Legacy

A childhood tragedy had pitted CEO Adam Bartlett against all things medical. But when he learned his blood could save a little boy's life, Adam turned to nurse Leigh Peters—his first love—to help see him through the emotional procedure. Were the sparks that flew between them just an echo from the past…or the promise of a future?

#1600 WHERE YOU LEAST EXPECT IT—Tori Carrington

No one in Old Orchard knew that teacher Aidan Kendall was a man on the run. Aidan hadn't intended to stay in the small town…until he met Penelope Moon. The mystical beauty made Aidan believe in magic and miracles. But would their love survive when the danger on his heels caught up with him?

#1601 TYCOON MEETS TEXAN!—Arlene James
The Richest Gals in Texas

Avis Lorimer wanted a no-strings affair to go with her London vacation. Wealthy businessman Lucien "Luc" Tyrone was only too happy to oblige the soft-spoken Texas beauty. It was the perfect fling—until Luc decided he wanted Avis not just for the moment, but forever. Convincing Avis, however, was another matter!

#1602 DETECTIVE DADDY—Jane Toombs

A Michigan storm had landed a very pregnant—very much in labor—Fay Merriweather on the doorstep of police detective Dan Sorenson's cabin. After a tricky delivery, Dan was duty-bound to see that Fay and her baby got the care they needed. He never intended to actually fall for this instant family.…

SSECNM0204